THE BELLIGERENT ENTITY

KEV CARTER

PLEASE VISIT MY WEB SITE

www.fancyacoffee.wixsite.com/kev-carter-books

ISBN: 9798854801409

CHAPTER ONE

It was a sunny day and the fields were green and lush, the beautiful landscape was lost on them, both running and playing together like young friends do no worries and not a mind in the world. The future held wonders and dangers but they did not care, right now they were racing each other to the other end of this field.

"Come on Richard I am winning" she shouted as she forged ahead of her friend, breathing heavy and excited at the thought of getting to the far dry stone wall before him. But her excitement turned to dread as he ran past her laughing and shouting.

"Come on Stephanie" he said laughing and leaving her in his wake as he pelted past and jumped on the wall before her looking back and watching her catch up. She was breathing heavy but didn't give up, when she made it and gasped for breath saying as she did.

"I let you win so you didn't start crying"

"Whatever you say, you big girl" he smiled down at her and then took a deep breath of the country air. She lifted herself up onto the wall and sat next to him, getting her breath back, she noticed something in between stones of the wall, reaching in she fished it out. Holding it up she looked at it, a small stone, well worn but it had a distinctive shape of a heart.

"Oh wow look, it's a heart made of stone, it's so beautiful"

"It must be a sign" Richard said looking as she held it up in front of her admiring it.

She smiled and turned to him holding out the stone.

"I want you to have this it is my heart and will always be yours keep it safe and never let it go, you must promise me this forever and ever" she placed the stone in his hand and wrapped his fingers around it to make sure.

"I will guard it with my life, and when we are older and together I will give it back to you"

"Thank you and I hope we are friends for ever until we die don't you?"

"Yes of course" he put the stone in his pocket and put his arm around her.

"I don't want to go back to school tomorrow do you?" she said regaining her composure.

"Not really, I would much rather stay here, I like it here"

"Yeah so do I let's just run away together because I will be going away to that stupid school and have to live with me dad and won't see you much anymore" her face was genuinely sad as she spoke.

"Hey we will always be friends and we will always keep in touch" he looked at her and put his arm around her shoulders and pulled her into him she liked it and felt comfortable there.

"When we leave school we shall run away together, will you wait for me?"

"Stephanie I will always wait for you because you are my best friend" he said smiling down at her and she smiled back at him.

Looking up he listened to a sky lark it was high up in the sky and then started to drop it was still singing until it hit the grass then stopped.

"Let's go to the top of the tower what do you say?" Richard said enthusiastically

"It scares me going up inside it; I think evil spirits live there" she said shaking her head.

"You daft bugger there's nowt to be afraid of come on" he jumped from the wall and walked off towards the stone tower that was situated on top of the hill; it was an old tower and looked like a large chess piece. There was a stone stairway inside and the views from the top were breathtaking, scanning over north Yorkshire and it was a popular place for walkers. She reluctantly followed him slowly at first then she dashed forward and caught him up, they both climbed over the wooden five bar gate and onto the road.

Looking both ways they ran over and started to ascend up the steep incline to the top, it then levelled out and there stood the stone tower. It didn't take then long being ten years old gave them a lot of energy. Stephanie looked at the foreboding structure with dread she didn't like it. Richard was eager to get in and up the stone steps and out to the top.

"Come on Steph lets go" He said smiling and taking her hand leading her to the base of the cold solid stoned fifty foot monster that lived high up on this hill. Looking up to the top it was a cold frightening sight to her and she started to feel dizzy and strange. Richard led her by the hand and went into opening and started to carefully climb the staircase inside. It was pitch black except for the odd slit of an opening in the wall every now and then.

"I bet this was where they fired their arrows from at the attacking force" he said excited as they went round and further up.

"Did you hear that, did you feel it" Stephanie said scared and gripping his hand tight.

"No what did you hear; we are almost there now come on keep hold of my hand"

"I'm scared Richard lets go back please"

"Almost to the top you will be fine then come on" he pulled her and eventually they could see the light from the opening at the top they carefully emerged and stood up looking out over the stone battlement and across the magnificent view.

Stephanie felt strange she could feel a pressure pressing down on her it was uncomfortable and she didn't understand it she became light headed and she felt dizzy and sick. She stood back a little and felt unsteady then had to sit down.

"I feel strange" she said becoming worried and scared.

"Hey, what's wrong, are you ok?" Richard knelt down by her said and took her hand it was cold and she was shivering her eyes rolled back in her head and he could see the whites of her eyes swelling in the sockets. She began to shake and convolute uncontrollably. Suddenly she screamed and started to shake her head from side to side. Then she was still and weeping curling up in the foetus position. Scared and worried Richard looked about, the day had suddenly become dark, it was a strange darkness like a thick fog moving about and circling the tower. He didn't know what to do looking frantically down he could see no one about they were alone. he knelt down with Stephanie and held her in his arms they both closed their eyes then suddenly there was a loud crack in the air it was like a giant whip being unleashed above their heads. Keeping their eyes closed they both shook with fear until Richard mustered the nerve to look up. He could hear screams but not see anything it was pitch black all around him, dropping his head again and closing his eyes he held onto Stephanie.

The whole tower was trembling and vibrating right from its foundations.

Scared and shaking he closed his eyes tighter, he held his breath but had to let it out to breath he didn't know what to do and squeezed Stephanie tight towards him.

He could feel her shaking and her body twitching violently in his arms. Becoming panicky he began to feel himself shaking also but suddenly the heavy atmosphere seemed to lift around him. Taking a deep breath of courage he lifted his head once more, the sky was bright and sunny again the dark fog had gone. He stood up and looked down across the landscape it was as it was before, like nothing had happened.

"Steph come on we got to get out of here lass" he said and pulled her up onto her feet.

Blindly following him they quickly but carefully descended back down the staircase. They didn't say anything but ran as fast as they could away and back down to the road. Dashing cross it they ran into the field and didn't look back.

It was not until they were almost home at Stephanie's house did they stop and catch their breath. They sat on the wooden bench outside her back garden and both regained some composure.

“Are you alright, you looked like some sort of zombie up there?” Richard said to her.

“What happened I don’t remember I was in another place another time it was horrible, olden times where people were hanging from trees by their necks and this dark cloud thing was everywhere it was dreadful, people were screaming and I could not move but I could see it” she shook her head and had to stop herself from crying out.

“Bloody hell, I don’t know, glad we are away from that bloody tower, not going there again” Richard told her and held her hand for comfort.

“Nor me, I told you it was evil, me mum always said it had an evil past that place”

“Well we will never go there again or tell anyone about it, they won’t believe us anyway”

“My mum would be mad if I told her, she always said stay away from it”

“I am sorry I took you there, I didn’t realise” Richard squeezed her hand and she smiled at him then looked worried.

“I hope I have not been cursed” she said looking him straight in the eye.

"No we got away quickly I think you will be fine, and I will always protect you Lass you know that no matter what" he smiled at her and she smiled back, knowing he meant it.

"We will laugh about this when we get older won't we, what we did as kids and all that"

"Well it was no laughing matter but I am sure we will yes"

She leant forward and kissed him on the cheek and he went red and smiled at her, she squeezed his hand and sighed out.

"I am going to miss you when we move to in with my dad and different schools, I have to stay there and only come home on holidays" she looked dejected and saddened.

"We will always have a strong bond, you and me nothing will ever come between us, let's make a promise about that"

"I promise" she said smiling at him

"I promise too" he said smiling back at her.

She looked back in the direction of the tower and was silent for a moment, then turning to Richard she said.

"What happened up there it was horrible and I still feel funny inside" she looked worried and he thought she was going to cry, putting his arm around her he said comfortingly.

"Whatever it was is now gone, It can't hurt you every again and we are definitely not going back up there ever"

"I never want to go back up there, and hope I am not cursed"

“No, no what do you say that it is a silly thing to say, no one has cursed you”

“My mum says they can she knows about these things she can do strange things like make you well when you are sick and get plants and herbs for the house that always keep things away like bugs and make the house feel fresh and safe it is strange sometimes”

“It’s called air freshener my mum uses it too, and fly killer” he said innocently but seriously.

“No not like that, she is one with the earth she says, I hear her chanting sometimes and she has tons of books on spells and stuff”

“Wow, I didn’t know your mum was into that stuff, like sorcery and all that, can she cast spells?” he was genuinely interested and wanted to know more.

“No she isn’t bad or evil she just knows things about stuff” she shook her head and was lost and could not explain because she didn’t understand it herself.

“Wow that so interesting Steph, I will never look at your mum the same again”

“Please don’t say I have told, she will not be happy if she knows I have told you”

“I promise your secret is safe with me” he smiled at her and she smiled back, she felt better now and looked ahead and decided never to look back towards that stone tower again.

They sat in silence for a short while before they decided to head back and go home, it was a sad time for them because they were going to separate schools now and would not see each other until holidays. They hugged and Stephanie cried. Richard held her and promised they would always be friend. He watched her walk towards her front door and she turned wiped her eyes and waved to him. He waved back and she went in closing the door behind her, it was silent all around all of a sudden and he had a strange feeling.

He stood looking at the door for a moment then sadness came over him, he pulled himself away and headed off home he was miserable and his body language showed it, his head was bowed and he dug his hands deep into his pockets. She was his best friend and he was still scared about what had happened although he did not understand it. But most of all he had this strange feeling he would not see her again, it was an overwhelming feeling and he didn’t like it one bit, he held the stone in his hand all the way home.

Stephanie had a similar feeling when she was sat in her room, she felt strange and just sat there looking at the wall, and it seemed to calm her for some reason. Her mother called her down for some food shortly after and she went down unenthusiastically she ate in silence and her mother knew instantly there was something wrong.

“What is a matter with you?” she asked as she was sat across from her at the dinner table.

“Nothing, just sad and worried about that school and going to stay with daddy” she said without stopping chewing and eating her food.

“Don’t be silly, it’s a great school, you will make lots of new friends and be away from this dreary place, you would like that wouldn’t you?” she said with a smile of encouragement.

“I like it here mommy and I have friends here” she looked up still chewing some bread.

“This area is no good for you honey you need to move and enjoy other places and friends and experiences you will be fine, you come home at holidays and we can set off on adventures when you do, that will be great wont it?” she tried to sound uplifting but she was hurt seeing her daughter so sat an down. She didn’t really understand because they had talked it all over before and it was settled and Stephanie seemed fine with it. Sensing something was wrong she looked into her daughters eyes and could see and feel the sadness but also something else, the fear, fear of something she was holding back.

“I suppose mummy” she said with a little forced smile.

“What is wrong, I know something is wrong, it is not just you moving away to another school is it, tell me Stephanie, tell me what is causing you to fear inside so much”

“It’s nothing I am fine, just sad at leaving my friends and this place”

“Don’t lie to me child I can feel it, I can see into your soul I know you are scared what has happened, please tell me I will not be mad but I need to know baby” she stared at her daughter intensely and could read any sign, any gesture and knew her inside and out like no other mother could know their child.

“You will be mad, I know you will be mad mummy” Stephanie said looking down at the table in silence, she had lost her appetite and now knew her mother knew something was wrong and would find out for sure she always did.

Reaching out she took her daughters hand and felt the vibrations and feelings from it she felt the tense and the increased heat beat she felt the palm becoming clammy she knew something was wrong, so quietly and sympathetically she asked Again.

“Tell me what is wrong child you can tell me you must tell me so I can help you”

Looking up Stephanie bit her bottom lip for a moment then took a deep breath she knew it was useless to resist her mother knew everything and had a way to get it out of her.

“I was with Richard today, we went to the fields” she looked at her mother for a reaction knowing she disapproved of him, but she stayed calm.

“Baby I do not mind you having friends, but please we agreed you would stay away from that Richard Cushing, his mother is an angle but I know there is something not right within that child, something that is going to erupt in violence. Please stay away from him, we talked about it before didn’t we?” she gently squeezed her little hand.

“Yes mummy but we are friends and he is very nice and he protects me at school from bullies and helps me with things and walked me home when them boys were going to beat me up, he walked with me and backed them off” she told her as if it was going to change everything and it would all be alright now. But she could see her mother was not impressed and it unnerved her somewhat.

“You are not telling me everything are you, what is wrong?” she said calmly but firmly and Stephanie knew she had no choice but to tell because her mother would be relentless and get it out of her in the end.

“Please don’t be mad, please mommy” Stephanie said before she had to tell.

"I promise I will not be mad but tell me what is wrong I can feel it and know something is eating you inside you have to let these things go or they will destroy you"

"We went to the tower on the hill, and when we got there I saw things and felt strange but I am alright now and we ran away" she said it in one breath then held her breath until she had to let it out again. Her mother looked at her with loving eyes but fear on her face. She silently and slowly stood from the table and turned away from her daughter. The look or worry and dread on her face she wanted to hide from her. Putting her hand up to her mouth she sighed out and shook her head. Then regained her composure and turned with a smile and looked at the worried Stephanie looking at her with worry in her eyes.

"Ok baby, now I am not going to be angry with you but you must promise me never, and I mean never go to that place, the tower again will you do that for mommy?" she came and knelt down by her daughters side and took her little trembling hand in hers.

"Yes mommy I promise, I don't ever want to go there again"

"Good girl, so tonight you set off on a new adventure and you can forget all about it can't you, so finish your food and let's make sure you are packed up"

“I am sorry mommy I am sorry” she said a little relieved she was not being told off”

Her mother hugged her and she noticed she was holding her tighter than normal and longer than she normally did.

“It’s ok my angle it’s ok”

Stephanie could not rest she was sat on her bed and was ready to go she was anxious and she heard her mother chanting and moving about a lot. She heard her on the phone making sure he dad was coming to pick her up. She heard more movement and more rushing about. She was confused because her mother normally was quiet and didn’t make much noise. Looking at her two small suitcases and not understanding why she had to leave and go live with her father it confused her and upset her. Her heart sank when she heard the car pull up and tears welled up in her eyes. The room door opened and her mother stood there and came to her giving her a long hug and reassured her it was only for a while and not for ever. They both cried and both told each other they will miss them. Eventually she left the house and went to her father car, he was waiting stood by the cars side with the door open for her with a big smile. She got in and her parents were chatting for a short while then her father got in the car and they drove away. Looking out of the back window she waved to her mother who was crying and waving back to her. Her Father was talking to her but she didn’t hear him she was transfixed on the image of her getting further away and smaller she had a very weird horrid feeling she would never see her again, she didn't like it but somehow excepted it. Not understand any of it she just waved one last time until they were far away and that was it, he mother was gone. She turned and faced the front smiling and nodding to her father as he spoke to her but she didn't hear him and was dazed and felt drugged and subdued.

That night the storm hit from nowhere, it was not forecast but it was fierce and violent. Richard laid in his bed his hands behind his head listing to it and watching the flashing lighting up the night sky, he liked storms and this was a belter.

The tower stood in the dark being illuminated by the flashing of lightening and stood at the base was Stephanie's Mother; she was screaming up at the tower and holding out her arms. Shaking her head and ignoring the rain lashing down on her face and soaking her to the skin.

The more she chanted the ancient ritual, the more violent the storm became, she screamed in an old unused language she threw her arms out and up at the wall of this menacing stone monument.

"Leave my child alone you have no power over my child" she screamed and then spun around on the spot reciting an ancient language never heard for centuries. The lighting struck only feet away from her but she did not flinch. The whole structure of stone started to shake and rumble from deep within its foundations. It was moving it was shaking and the more she shouted the more it shook.

"Take me, leave my child you can't escape I will trap you forever with in this tower with my life take me, I demand you to take me and stay where you are" she screamed the words out and she looked up as mortar started to crumble and fall from the top, a stone shook loose and fell only inches from her it bounced and settle shaking on the ground. The storm was more violent than ever and the lighting stuck the tower splitting one side, an inch wide crack appeared and ran down to the foundations from the top.

"I condemn you to eternal darkness with my life as a seal to keep you there" her words seemed to bellow above the storms noise. Every time she spoke the tower shook and the earth around her vibrated with her words, she was drenched and cold she was shivering and exhausted but she carried on. She knew she had to because this thing was after her daughter she knew that and she knew it had to be contained and sealed down.

"Darkness of ancient history you have no power here you have no place in this time, I seal you to the depths of hell with my life force" she touched the cold wet stone and screamed with agony as the pain rushed through her. Lightening struck the tower again and she screamed out again with words not spoken for thousands of years she knew this was the only way to stop this evil from attacking and taking her daughter. She was willing to sacrifice her own life to save Stephanie. A crack of thunder shook the whole hillside and shook her off her feet, she fell and looked up to see the bolt of lightning hit the tower splitting it in two and the top park of the battlement came crashing down on top of her she screamed out her final words and the spell was sealed moments before she was smashed and crushed under tons of stone. The whole tower shook and cracked the stone falling the sound of an unearthly evil crying out and trying to escape but the seal was strong she had given her life to lock it and the tower collapsed in a heap of stone the lightning struck it and smashed the stones to pieces the ground sunk and the tower was devoured and was taken down along with the body of Stephanie's mother she had sacrificed herself to seal the evil darkness within its pit within the towers rubble. The storm faded and the night became still the tower was gone.

Just a pile of stones remained no one would know the truth and no one would ever to think of looking down under the foundations to seek out an evil more powerful than anything on the planet. No one would know the hidden covered body of the woman there was sealing it and holing it captive with her ancient power and understanding. It would stay like that for eternity. Or would there be another who would understand the power in time. Years passed and things were forgotten the tower was no more than, a memory of local folk and they tell of a storm and it was destroyed by lighting. It is of no interest to anyone now just a pile of stone.

CHAPTER TWO

The music was much too loud in this night club; no wonder young people lost their hearing, it was over crowded and dark. He stood by the bat watching out for trouble, he knew the signs, the look. He was getting stared at by a large black man who was swaying in the corner glaring at him. He noted it and would be ready if anything started. It was getting to be the case of not the customers he had to worry about but the colleagues he worked with, three of them worked this club but the other two didn't like him and the feeling was mutual.

"Hay what can I get you" a friendly voice said from behind the bar while she had a moment. He knew who it was and it made him smile.

"Drunk, then take advantage of me I suppose" he said without looking back at her.

"Well I've done that before you are such an easy lay, why don't you play hard to get for a change you bloody tart" her voice was friendly and they were friends but no one had to know about it, not in that way anyway.

"I will try I really will honest" he said turning and smiling at her, his face then dropped "Shit I thought you were someone else hello Nina" he smiled again and she did the same.

“I will make you pay for that my lad” she winked and turned to serve some loud mouth shouting for service before the bar closed. He watched her tight athletic figure move away from him and had a lot of lovely happy and exciting memories about that body.

He walked through and out to the front area, on the door was the other two doormen; they paid him no attention when he came to the front for some air.

“Your Job is inside tonight Yorkie” one said not looking in his direction.

“Your job is to shut the fuck up and mind your own business” he said looking out into the street and taking a breath of fresh air. He knew they both didn’t like him and he also knew they were constantly reporting him to Big Dave the owner.

“One of these days I am going to open everything that is shut and shut everything that is open on you, you big mouthed cunt” the two of them both looked at each other then both of them looked at him. Turning and not bothering to waste his breath we walked back inside.

“Fucking arse wipe” the first one said to his friend who nodded in agreement.

“Well he is gone tonight I think, Dave believed what you told him”

“Really?” he smiled and felt satisfied that he had had a lie believed and it had the effect he was looking for. Less than half an hour later they both came on the inside knowing it was about time to close, the night had been relatively quiet but they knew that could change at any minute. Especially now it was chucking out time. The music stopped the DJ said goodnight and the lights came up. People moaned and looked around some were narrowing their eyes and staggering about drunk. Others were surprised who they were actually with now the lights had gone on, and some were just leaned against the wall not really knowing where they were, or how they got there, obliviously drunk.

“Come on lads chucking out time” Big Dave said, his size and large belly gave him his name these days but years ago he was a capable body builder and the name suited him in a more respected manner. He shouted out in a booming voice and told people to leave and go home. Two other men were leading people out and seeing them on their way down the road. The bar staff were clearing up and the place gradually emptied. A large black man was swaying about and looking at one of the bouncers with distaste in his eyes, then shouted.

“You, I don’t like you man” he said pointing to him and breathing in so his chest puffed out.

“I don’t like you either so we are quits, it’s time for you to go home big lad”

“You going to make me are you?”

“If I have to yes, be much easier for you to walk out of here though don’t you think” he stood his ground and looked this large figure of a man in the eye. His experience and his keep awareness he could see what was about to happen. The large man lurched forward with a punch which was ducked and avoided easily. The attacker staggered with his own momentum and then turned around and dashed forward with a lot of force and aggression.

“You fucking cunt” he shouted as he did.

But he was ready for him and delivered an uppercut so hard and correct it lifted the man’s head violently up and threw his whole body back. Quickly and smoothly he grabbed the man’s right arm and twisted it up his back and pushed him towards the door.

Stunned and dazed the black man was shuffled then marched out of the room to the front door, he was cursing as he was pushed out and the bouncer grabbed the little finger of the man’s right hand as he pushed him out and snapped it. This was something he had picked up knowing they would not be able to come back with a punch with a broken finger.

He was so drunk the man didn't realise at first then fell on the floor; he was till dazed and crawled away mumbling to himself as he did. He walked back inside when he saw the man was no longer a threat.

"Thanks for your help" he said sarcastically to his two colleagues, who both smirked and said nothing. The place was just about empty now and he had had enough he wanted to get home. Walking to big Dave he didn't have to say anything. Dave reached into his pocket and handed him some money. Counting it he put this into his own pocket and started to walk out.

"Think you won't be needed again Cushing" Dave shouted after him and smiled to the other two bouncers. It was obvious there was no love lost here and they didn't like each other. It suited Richard and he was going to leave it at that but inevitably one of the other bouncers had to say something.

"Good bye Yorkshire homo I would like to say it's been nice knowing you but it hasn't, so I won't" he laughed and his colleague joined in.

Richard turned around and caught the eye of the attractive Nina behind the bar she was shaking her head and pleading with him with her eyes to go and leave it.

"What the fuck are you going to do for a face when the elephant wants its arsehole back?"

It was then that it all erupted and Richard knew he had to hit hard and fast to stand a chance. He kicked one between the legs and brought him down then kneed him viciously in the face knocking him back with a split open nose and reeling on the floor. The second bouncer lunged towards Richard and ruby tackled him to the ground. They both rolled about and both trying to get the better of the other. Big Dave was striding over towards them and Richard caught his shape through his peripheral vision coming closer. He poked his attacker in the eye and head butted him but was not quite fast enough to get to his feet before Big Dave kicked him with full force in the head sending him rolling off and dazed.

The bar maids screamed and told them to stop, they all started coming round from the bar area and running up towards them.

"Stay fucking there" Dave turned and shouted at them stopping them all in their tracks. It was the few seconds Richard needed and he picked up a wooden stool and lashed out with it as Big Dave turned to face him. It caught him completely off guard and rocked his head back and his body followed he fell to the floor in a collapsed heap. Front teeth were missing and blood was coming from his mouth and a gash on his head. He was out cold and the women all screamed and didn't know what to do. Richard looked at the other two but they were both rolling about holding their heads and moaning. He staggered up to his feet and caught the eye of the

Nina again; she moved her head to the door in a silent gesture for him to get out. He didn't argue he shook his head and got his senses back then left the place.

Driving away minutes later in his Land Rover Defender 110 he cursed and hit the steering wheel, he should have just left but could not resist it. They had not liked him for a while and just something about them bothered him, they had not seen eye to eye and it had just got worse and worse over time. It probably didn't help he was sleeping with Big Dave daughter and if he ever found out he would hire someone to take Richard out, he knew a lot of bad and nasty people. Well he thought time to move on, this town had become boring and it was time to leave he made the decision to pack up and get out. Pulling up to his small one bed room flat he locked up his car and walked into his place. As always he was met with love and happiness from his golden retriever dog Max. He was his best friend and the only thing he trusted in this world. They wrestle on the floor and play fought for a few minutes then Richard stood and looked down at his happy friend wagging his tail and looking back up at him, loyal and always there no matter what.

"Well shagger, it's time for us to move on old friend" he shook his head to clear the dizziness and went to take a shower. He let the water cascade down his strong muscle body and let the dirt of the night the sweat the blood wash away. He felt better and refreshed as he left to dry off then a knock came to his door and Max went over growling. Richard walked up to the door and listened tying the towel around his waist. A small knock came again, he looked at Max who had stopped growling and just sat there which told him he must know who is there.

"Yeah what do tha want?" Richard asked

"It's me, open up quickly you don't have a lot of time" a woman's voice told him with a degree of urgency. He recognised it as Nina and opened the door quickly; she rushed in past him and looked scared. He looked outside and then closed and locked the door behind her.

"What the hell are you doing here; he will know you are gone?" Richard told her, but there was no fear or urgency in his voice.

"He is on his way to the hospital with the other two, one might lose an eye, he is going to put a contact out on you Richard, and he will do it he has done it before he knows people, bad people you have to get away now, tonight" she sounded genuinely scared and concerned.

"Well I was thinking the same thing actually, bloody southerners" he said walking back into the room while Max was waiting for a pet from this woman friend but never got it so he went and sat down and just observed from the corner.

"They just didn't like you, I think they were jealous of you and saw you as a threat" she said following him to the bed room.

"How long do I have do you think?" he said turning to face her.

"They will keep him in overnight I would say but tomorrow he will make some calls and you are dead meat son, these men don't mess about, you have to get away"

"So I have until the morning then?" he asked looking at her attractive and firm sexy body.

"Forget it lover, no, you have to get away it's been fun and all that but if my dad found out..."

Richard smiled at her and undid the towel it dropped to the floor and he stood there naked looking at her. She shook her head and backed away holding out her hands.

"No way Richard it's over lover and you have to move on"

Richard walked over to her and put his hand behind her head pulling her face towards his and kisses her deeply on the mouth, she didn't resist just moaned out and put her hands on his body running them all over as she kissed him back passionately. They fell back on the bed and made love with passion and vigour like they always did. Both naked and panting they were on their backs looking at the ceiling when they had finished.

“You are a complete Bastard you know that?” she said not looking at him.

“You have to be to survive these days love” he said sighing out and turning to face her resting his elbow on the bed and supporting his head in his hand. She turned and faced him looking into his blue eyes and asked.

“What will you do, where will you go, back up north?” she asked with more feeling in her voice and eyes as she looked at him.

“Probably I have had enough of southern hospitality”

“Well you didn’t help; you make it clear you don’t like people so they resent you for it”

“Say what I like and like what I say”

“What’s that a Yorkshire saying I suppose”

“Aye Lass it is that” he said in his best Yorkshire accent smiling at her

“Bloody weirdo you are, but I am going to miss you, she sighed out and shook her head, you must promise me you are going to get away I am serious about my dad he will have people out looking for you”

“I don’t doubt it, I am going to miss you as well you’re a grand lass” he leaned over and kissed her again she smiled and kissed him back they both hugged and lay together and closed their eyes. It was a last moment of their time together and it had been an enjoyable time for them both. But they both now knew it was over and they had to move on.

She left less than an hour later and Richard set his alarm for three house time he was going to get some sleep then pack up and go.

He fell asleep quickly but it was a troublesome sleep, Max came by his side and watched his master toss and turn in his bed, moaning and rocking his head. He could not see what he was dreaming but it was so real to Richard. The tower was back looming above him the stone harsh and cold against his skin as he was pushed against it.

His childhood memories flooding back, Stephanie running in a field he was chasing her they both ran past the Tower and then she were gone. He searched round for her but the fields had turned black then red and it rained, it rained red blood all over him he screamed but no sound was heard. The tower spun it turned and turned and he became dizzy. The tower was collapsing it was falling he was running up inside the tower round and round then suddenly he was at the top looking over the top and lost his balance he was plunged over the edge and falling, falling to the ground.

Suddenly he awoke in a sweat and panting, Max barking at him and wagging his tail, looking around the room he sighed out as he realised it had been a dream. Maybe the kick in the head had caused it he didn't know but it was so real and so strange. He had not thought about Stephanie for a while and when she never answered his letters he never saw her again. But he felt strange now some feeling deep inside him had not felt before. It had been almost thirty years since he was playing in the fields with Stephanie, his Family moved back to Yorkshire when he was eleven and all contact was lost. So why was he dreaming about it now, he sat up on the edge of the bed and looked at his faithful companion sitting next to him. He reached down and stroked him causing the dog to take it as a signal to jump on the bed and join him. Looking at his watch on the side he could see he had been asleep for two hours and decided that was enough it was time to leave and time to get out of this place.

Max stayed on the bed and laid in the warmth where his master had been laid, his scent was strong there and it gave him comfort he was content to stay here while Richard packed up things and got ready to move on. Leaving a note for his landlady saying he was moving down to London just to throw them off a little if anyone called round, he double checked the place and then took the three bags he had packed all his worldly possessions in and went to the door. Max followed and would go where ever his master lead, stepping outside he looked around it was quiet and still everyone were asleep and the night was crisp and fresh locking the door he posted the keys and they both went to his land Rover.

Moments later he was driving out of this town and away, but where he didn't know, that was until something happened that shocked him Max let out a howl, something he had never done before, Richard looked back where the dog was on the back seat. Max started to act strange, he seemed to cough then struggle to get his breath. The dog sat up on the back seat and shook his head in confusion.

"You, alright there big lad? Richard asked talking to his dog like he always had done. He slowed down and pulled to a stop by the side of the road. He turned and looked with concern at his trusted dog. He had never seen him act like this before. The dog's very large bulk and size heaved as if he was retching then stopped. He looked at his master with blood shot eyes.

"Max, what is it, what's wrong?"

The dog then lifted its large powerful head and howled like a wolf baying at the moon. Over and over it howled and Richard looked about all around to see what was happening to see if any danger was approaching. He reached over and put his hand on his dogs head, he could feel the animal shaking. Concern made its self felt and Richard turned in his seat reaching back to take hold of his dog, give him some comfort. Max let out another long howl and then looked at his master, staring at him intensely. Richard looked back into them eyes and knew something was very wrong. He had not seen his dog like this before it was strange and worrying, visions of his childhood flashed into his head and he didn't know why.

****

The ruin was quiet, laying there like a dead monster, killed some time ago and now just a dormant reminder of what it used to be. But today it is stirring something is causing ripples of movement. The horrific secrets it holds the torturous past it hides maybe rising or is it something else, is it the porthole it covers, is it something else using the exit into this word? Whatever it is causing it to shake to move and it is getting stronger and more violent. The body of stones move, they scatter. The whole area around it is unnaturally silent. The place is dead, desolate and arid. But the Towers ruins have come alive it is moving, something is rising deep from within; a secret it holds is bursting out. It is giving up and spewing out something from its deep dark depths. Suddenly the surface is broken, like a great monster it is coming out of the earth of the darkness. Rising up the whole structure lifting slowly up and moving out of the earth and onto the land where it once stood. It was a strange and unearthly sight. The Tower looked menacing it was back now and you would never have known it had just rose from the dark hole in the hillside only minutes earlier. Something was wrong, something was very wrong, the silence and the atmosphere was unnatural. Not of this world, something had brought this Tower back and something was stirring once again, there was a scream a blood curdling horrific scream. Somewhere in that Tower someone was feeling the grip and torment of something evil. It was a scream full of pain and anguish, a woman who was hurt, tortured and desperate. The echo of that scream bounced off the walls of that Towers interior. Somewhere in the depth of that stone structure was a soul trying to escape trying to break out. It was fighting with superhuman strength and a determination stronger than life its self, breaking away from the perpetual darkness that encased it. There was one man who would know who that scream came from, one man would understand, but that man was not here. That man was Richard Cushing; he would instantly know who that desperate cry for help came from. The screams grew louder and were filled with dread; it was a last ditched attempt to break free from the grip the darkness had hold of. This was the last and only chance. The agonising screams persisted and the area stayed still no one ever came here, no one wanted too. It was a void in the land, like a vacuum of space. The Tower stood and looked like it had never been away, just sat there harbouring the torment and evil it had inside. The screams continued and the fight of good and evil persisted inside. Deep within its soul that Tower was a battle ground and the screams were the cries of a woman would go unheard unless Richard could somehow hear them and come. That was the only chance she had, it took all her strength and power to get here and now she had to find him and bring him to her, but she was weakening and the blanket of evil was encasing her from all sides.

The screams rang out the torture continued and the monumental stone stood solid. There was a crash of noise a roar of a voice that deep and over powering, like a demon cursing. Something was crushing this woman's defences down and she was in trouble, she didn't have much time and then she would be gone cast into hell never to be seen or heard on earth again. Her screams would be enjoyment for the evil that awaited her in the darkest pit of hell fire.

****

He didn't know why and he had no idea what was going on but something compelled him to go back to the Tower, he had dreamed of it, he now had flash backs to it. Max was staring at him intensely reaching out he put his hand on the dogs head and he got a jolt of pain and a vision like he had never experience. A woman screaming at him, asking him for help that woman was Stephanie he was sure of it, older and mature now but it was her. What did this mean? Why was it happening he had no idea but he knew one thing and that was where he had to go and go now?

Not happy he was racing quickly and headed out towards the bypass and up to where he must now go. He stopped only once to fill up with diesel and then head off again. Max stirred a few times but was asleep and seemed none the worse for the experience. Going as fast as he could turning off the road and heading towards the dirt track he noticed it was untouched and forgotten, he drove up the over grown dirt road that lead to the Tower, the Land Rover making easy of the uneven surface. Max shifted and sat up, he became alert and was back to his old self, he knew there was danger and he could sense it strongly.

Richard slowly drove through grassed area and was amazed at the sight that greeted him; he stopped and looked up in amazement at the Tower. Silent and in twilight it seemed even more evil than before he stared at it and it was like it stare back at him and they both remembered each other. Double checking the area he looked everywhere and all around his vicinity. The Tower seemed to loom and have a presence all of its own. He slowly got out of the defender and let Max out the back. The dog came by his side instantly and they both edged towards the formidable and eerie sight that was in front of them.

He froze when he heard the scream, it was Stephanie he knew it, somewhere inside that horror of a place was his true friend. He ran towards the place and Max loyally trotted by his side. Richard shouted out Stephanie's name. He stood listening but it was silent. He signalled Max to look about which the dog freely did sniffing the ground and looking everywhere.

They both stood there, Richard watching his dog and would act on its reaction. The hairs lifted on the dogs back and a low growl came from deep inside. Richard knew it was a warning growl and he was instantly put on alert. Max was sniffing the ground then he shook his head like he had just got a bad nauseating smell in his nostrils. Richard turned to check his surroundings, nothing was here but it didn't feel right it just was not a natural place to be. Then the whole place shook Max had to steady himself otherwise he would have been thrown off his feet. Richard reached out and put his hand on the wall to steady him otherwise the same fate would have been upon him. The whole place creaked and the stones began to crack, looking like they were being compressed. He then heard it, a scream a cry for help.

"Stephanie" Richard shouted he spun around searching for some sign where it was coming from. Max growled again and started to bark, the whole place was slipping back, being pulled back into the darkness below. It was shaking them off their feet and they were struggling to keep stood upright. The scream came again it was louder and nearer Richard could see nothing he desperately searched and didn't know what to do. The tower was sinking lowering back down into the earth darkness befell the whole place and he could not see anything. It was deep down now and only the top battlement was showing he looked around not knowing what was happening. He backed off and was going to head away then turned and saw Max lagging behind he seemed to he weighed down. As Richard got out onto firm ground he turned and pulled at Max dragging him out of the top towers opening. He was dragging his dog but also something else, someone else. He could see the arms of a woman around Max's neck Max fought and with his immense strength powered out of the Tower and dragged the naked woman with him. The stone work seemed to groan and twist as it was pulled back into the hole and back down into the darkness and abyss below. The stones falling and the ground shaking has it disappeared bit by bit slowly falling out of sight and being engulfed by the land this one last time?

Max was panting and Richard reached down lifting the bewildered woman up in his strong arms not looking back he and Max dashed for the defender. Opening the door he placed the woman carefully on the back seat and Max jumped in being careful to avoid trampling her as she curling up on the seat. He quickly got in he knew there was no danger from this woman this woman was Stephanie.

He looked back and doubled checked then glanced over at where the Tower had been only minutes earlier. He looked at Max who was looking back at him they locked eyes for a moment then he started the Engine and turned on his lights. He was confused and bewildered but just knew he had to get away from this place. Not understanding or believing what he had just seen he shook his head and breathed out several times regaining his composer. It was dark and he had memories of this place from when he was young before he moved away. He didn't know why he was thinking of Stephanie tonight but obviously there was the reason laid on the back seat. She is much older but he knew instantly who it was, he would never forget that girl.

CHAPTER THREE

Driving quickly Richard got away from this hell on earth, this little bit of darkness from the other side. He didn't look back again there was no need too. He didn't fully understand what was happening but his main concern right now was to get Stephanie away and safe. It was still dark and the roads were not too busy, he slowed down and headed away, he glanced back and could see Max had protectively wrapped himself around Stephanie. She was breathing but seemed frail and looked beaten and ill. Her hair had looked matted and raggedy the bruises and swelling on her face and body were well established. Headed out towards the main road and out of town he drove away and breathed out as he got further away and the distance grew larger from that place. He knew of a trusted bed and breakfast about an hour away he had used it many times and they knew him there and didn't ask any questions. He drove steady and periodically glanced back at the sleeping curled up figure that was Stephanie. She looked like a frail beaten lady at the moment. Max was being very protective and he kept her warm as they drove on their way. The memories flashing back to him of when they were children he was confused and somewhat bewildered, he had seen something tonight that was amazing and unbelievable, but he somehow knew that the woman on his back seat was most definitely Stephanie who had had not seen for over twenty five years.

Pulling up to one of the far cabins in the courtyard Richard got out and ran to the main building, he was not in there long they knew him when he used to work as handy man here, he was given the key post haste. He came quickly back and went into the end cabin room. Turning the light on Richard took a quick cautionary look in and then came back and let Max out of the back. The dog walked off and did what dogs do when they are in a new area; he marked his spot and checked for any danger. Reaching in Richard lifted the sleeping Stephanie from the back and safely took her into the room. He laid her on the bed and put a blanket over her. Going to lock and secure his Vehicle he pulled a bag from the back shouted Max back in and they went into the cabin closing and locking the door behind them. Richard got Max some water in a bowl and gave him some food from the bag he had brought in. It was dog meat wrapped in a plastic roll, breaking this in two he fed his dog, who welcomed it and devoured it quickly.

He watched as Stephanie stirred but didn't awaken, so he got some food himself and had a shower; Max lay by the door and kept guard. Richard took two small wedges from his bag and placed these tightly under the door so no one could open it. He was dressed in just his lose bottoms and then switched the small kettle on which was on a table with complimentary tea and a few cheap biscuits. Gently sitting down on the bed he reached out and touched Stephanie's head. It was warm and she was breathing steady she seemed at peace and resting well. He looked down at her face, it was gaunt she had obviously lost weight. She looked vulnerable he gently stroked her forehead and could see at her weak state. Glancing over to Max he could see the dog had settled down he looked back to Stephanie and smiled seeing her eyes were open and she was looking at him. She shook like a shiver then sat up hugging him tightly. Nothing was said for a moment they just held and Richard put his arms around her to make her feel safe and secure. They both knew despite not seeing each other all this time, he would battle anything to keep her secure.

"I am sorry, what can, I do, what the hell was all that tonight?" he said in a low voice.

"Keep me safe, keep me, don't let them get to me again, I would rather die" her voice faltered and he held her tighter.

"No one or nothing will ever hurt you, I will be by your side to make sure, I promise you this, we both will" Stephanie looked over at Max who was looking up at her and they made eye contact for a few moment.

“It was devastating, I was so wrong, never knew such power” Shaking she buried her head into his shoulder and controlled her erratic breathing.

“You are safe now I will not let anything harm you” Richard tried to sound reassuring but it was not his strong point, but he tried despite his confusion.

“You don’t understand, it is coming and they want me back, they will not stop and I can no longer stop them” She pulled away and looked into his eyes. He could see she was crying and her face was battered and full of fear and dread.

“I will be here and protect you Lass, calm down nothing will get to you I promise you that, I will fight them with the last bit of power I have me and Max, you are secure”

She shook her head and bowed it putting her hand to her face she rubber her eyes, looking across to Max who had stood up and was walking over to her. He sat next to the bed and she reached down to stroke him, a little smile came across her face. Richard watched them for a moment it seemed to calm her then looked around the room for no apparent reason, he did this a lot and it was habit just to make sure all was well.

“My power is gone ripped away from me like someone pulling my fingernails out” she turned and looked at him. She seemed to be searching his face then she leaned forward and kissed him gently on the lips.

"I will keep you safe Lass" He said locking eye contact with her, confused and worried.

"I know you will try but I do not know if we can win this, I thank you for coming and getting me but I have put you in mortal danger, I am so sorry but you and Max were my only, my one and only, chance of escape from the pain and torment"

"I don't understand, what is happening what is this all about, I'm sorry..."

"It is not your fault, ripped me right out, were pounded down and could do nothing to prevent it. Trapped under, the only part of me that had not succumbed was my connection to Max that was the only reason I was able to escape, it took all my strength and willpower. But now I have nothing, everything is gone. She bowed her head and sobbed again, Richard held her tight and showed her comfort she gladly accepted it and sunk her head into his broad chest, wrapping her arms around him.

"What do you mean connection to Max?" He was baffled and his curiosity was now getting the better of him, until now he had just accepted all this.

"There is so much you will not understand and so much you will not believe, when my mother died that horrid night I had the most terrifying nightmare. It took me many years to understand my gift my power"

"What are you talking about what the hell is happening here?" Richard suddenly had taken in what he had just seen and experience and it all hit him like a ton of bricks.

"You must go back and must remember"

"Go back where, what is going on Stephanie?"

"My mother was a strong and very powerful woman; she sacrificed herself to save me and mankind for that matter. I grew strong and learned my craft over the years"

"You are talking bollocks to me tell me lass what is going on how come that bloody tower was there then not there, why did I have a nightmare about you what happened to Max?" he said it all in one long breath then breathed in deeply.

"I felt I was strong enough to avenge and see my mother one last time, I gave you the dog, Max, so I would have a tie to you and I am so glad you were susceptible enough to see it"

"I found Max he was a stray" Richard suddenly became defensive and looked at his woman he was not sure of his own instinct was this really Stephanie?"

"He was left on your door step eighteen months ago, I watched you find him" she told him blankly and stared at him to judge his reaction.

"You knew where I was and left Max on my door step, why didn't you come and speak why didn't you show yourself?" he was confused but also intrigued

"You didn't seem in a good place at the time, and I was not ready I needed to prepare for my battle, I knew I would be able to find you through Max, they are exceptional animals dogs, I left him for you on your door step. When I knew I was ready to avenge my mother I tried but underestimated its power, I was trapped and the only way I was able to communicate was through the dog, it took me a long time to find him, but I did and I'm glad you could understand and read the signs" she smiled a weak smile and looked at him intensely.

Standing he walked around the room trying to make sense of it all he looked at Max who seemed content and totally unworried he looked over to Stephanie sat up looking at him.

"You never answered my letters, we moved back to Yorkshire when I was eleven to where I was born and that was it, never to see you again" he sighed out and shook his head.

"I am sorry, my father never gave me your letters he was a controlling man, and I was devastated when my mother died. It broke me emotionally and spiritually, but I managed to seek you out when I was powerful enough when I understood and controlled the gift my mother had passed on to me"

“What Power, you knew where I was and you never came to say hello?”

“Do you remember that last day that day we said we would always be friends, no matter what, we raced over that field and went to my house, you walked me home and we said we would never let anything come between us well do you keep your promises Richard, do you still have that same dignity and loyalty you had back then. The times you protected me at school from bullies and always helped me whenever I need it?” she had tears in her eyes and he realised he was the only and last chance she had. Suddenly all the doubt and all the scepticism was suppressed he was looking at the Stephanie of old his best friend and his child hood sweetheart. He nodded and came and sat next to her.

“Don’t worry you are protected now, and you have us, we will make sure...”

“Richard you do not understand, I have no power, nothing left I have been stripped of everything not only my will but my gift, my power, and my whole existence was destroyed” he could see now that this was paramount in her feelings and rooted in her very being.

He held her at arm’s length and looked her in the eye; she smiled a slight smile and held her tight, but reassuringly.

“I know you must have been through hell Stephanie, literally, but I can assure you that nothing will take you from me, nothing will ever beat me and take you again, I promise you this, and when a Yorkshire man gives his promise you can be sure it’s a bloody good one” he smiled and wanted to try and lighten her up a little and put her at ease somewhat. She stared at him blankly for a moment and he thought he had made a mistake and upset her, but her face finally cracked into a little smile and he smiled broadly back at her.

“You will never change my warrior, but what is coming for me will not be like anything before, it won’t like that I have escaped and it will hunt me down to drag me back, you are my only chance, I need you, you and Max” she glanced down at the dog looking up at her.

“Well you have a lot then don’t you, you look drained tried and like shite, why don’t you go get a shower and I will see what grub I have, while I make us a brew”

She shook her head and could not believe what she was hearing, his matter of fact attitude but then again she should have known, nothing fazed him even as a child and he handled whatever come to confront him. This time would be no different; she found it absolutely remarkable that she agreed and walked off into the shower. Her nerves were shattered her mind tormented but somehow when she looked at this man, she was calmed.

Richard made the tea and pulled some biscuits out of his bag and also a Tee shirt for Stephanie to wear, and some of his jogging pants. He knelt down and petted Max while the kettle was boiling and knew the dog was worried about Stephanie. He stood and walked to the window he looked out into the night. The dim light hanging on the outside did not do much to penetrate the oncoming darkness. He thought of himself as that light for a moment the all consuming darkness coming in and the light just standing there shining. The darkness not able to diminish it, it just keeps glowing defying the all powerful dark trying to encase it and damp it out. He would fight and never stop for what he believed, but what he saw tonight was beyond belief, everything happened to fast and the feeling was more instinct than anything else. Turning back into the room he made the drink then placed it on the side and waited for Stephanie to return. She eventually came back in with a large towel wrapped around her. Richard pointed to the joggers and tee shirt. She put the tee shirt on only leaving the joggers then came and sat on the bed.

He waited for her to settle and pushed her fingers through her short uneven cut hair pushing it all back, and she was saddened at how it felt.

She sighed out and sat across from him, he looked at her as he took a drink of his tea and ate two biscuits. She smiled and shook her head in disbelief.

"Never judge a book by its cover lass" he said knowing what she might be thinking.

"If I did not know you Richard Cushing I would think you were insane and just didn't grasp the situation we are now in" her voice had calmed and she seemed more composed.

"Worrying about something doesn't make it go away it just weakens you when you have to confront it. I don't know what might be coming and I will handle it the way I always do lass"

"I know you will I am sorry I have got you into this" she bowed her head and then reached over to take a drink.

"Never be sorry, I don't understand what is going on, it all seems unreal to me, but I know you need help and here it is, me" he tapped his own chest with two fingers.

"Thank you, I am trying to calm the experience, I am trying to compose myself, it is not easy but I will do it. I will be no help to you in the state I was in, I am free from their grasp, I will grow strong again and I will do all I can to help you, and try and explain"

"That's more like it, that's more like the Stephanie I knew" he smiled and was pleased inside he was hearing this, he needed her focused and brave.

She reached forward and took three of his biscuits from him and took another sip of her tea. Looking down at Max she saw the dog staring at her. She smiled and waved her hand in a gesture to tell him to leave her, all is well. The dog understood and walked back to the door and lay down on guard once again, but still looking at her.

"I do not know what to do, what to suggest, I have lost everything and can't go back to where I was, I have been dragged from my existence and plunged into this life"

"Where is that exactly?" he asked but she didn't hear him or ignored him.

"I thought I was strong enough to defeat it to see my mother again but I was sucked down and could not get out the only choice I had was to break back into this world through the porthole, the Tower it was the evil pulling me back you and Max arrived just in time, I have no other place to go, and I am afraid I may have released it"

"Well whatever this is, we will beat this together" he leaned forward and took her hand in his, she put her tea down and looked back.

She smiled and lunged forward and hugged him once again, she drew strength from him and knew this as the only man who could help her. She closed her eyes and took a deep breath.

“Thank you, thank you for coming for me” she said softly.

“I would go anywhere for you, will never let you down lass friends for life, remember?”

She pulled away and kissed him gently on the lips and smiled, she felt secure again and knew she now had a chance at least. He looked into her eyes and could see the hurt the torture but he could also see the glimmer of hope and the strength coming back.

“Are you hungry, do you want some food I don’t have much but we could muster something up for ya lass” He said glancing over at the bag he brought in.

She smiled and shook her head; she took another drink of her tea and sighed out. Rotating her neck she then tilted it back and forth and stretched her arms up and out. She looked tired and Richard knew she needed rest, rest and protection and that is what she will get tonight and every night from now on he found himself thinking.

“I don’t know where to go or what we will have now but I will do all I can to help, all I can, to do something positive my power is diminished but I will try my hardest to regain at least some of it, I promise” she suddenly looked a little concerned.

“Stephanie stop, whatever or whoever it is that comes, we will be together and I will not let any harm come to you”

“Thank you my Richard I am still confused myself” she smiled again at him

“You are knackered lass get some rest me and Max will be on guard rest of the night you will be safe here, you need some sleep” He then put his drink down and got off the bed. He pulled the sheets back and told her to get in. She did not argue and did as he suggested. The bed felt warm and welcoming and she suddenly felt very tired. He watched her snuggled down and then she looked up at him. Lifting her hand she held it out and he slid into the bed next to her. She fell asleep resting on his chest and he stayed there for her he watched her twitch and move in her sleep and knew she must be having a regress or something but he held her close and held her tight. He eventually fell asleep himself and knew they were safe with Max at the door. I had been one hell of a night he had no idea several hours before he would be in this situation whatever this situation was. He could see she was confused and mixed up; he played along for now but would want some proper answers when she had rested.

The area where the tower had been was calm the ground still but the place was not; there was blackness like no other surrounding it, deep thick darkness. Evil was here, the presence of absolute iniquity could be felt by them who knew. It was not just an evil spirit, or an entity or even a demon. This was something never seen before, it was not a living presence it was an evil from the darkest pit of hell. It had risen and was not going back until it had what it wanted. It didn't need to be a form it didn't need a shape. It was not a summoned warrior or a witch or a warlock it was just concentrated evil. It could move and command whatever it wanted and it had come to this place to get back what had escaped what had been taken it had come for Stephanie.

All the bad on this planet was under its command, all the evil that was here would bow to its demands. It had an army at its disposal but they just didn't know it yet. Control was its power and anything with a hint of badness or malevolence would be controlled and commanded. They would be under its will and they could do nothing about it, they would not know why they were doing what they were doing, but they would not be able to stop themselves, total control and loss of will power to do whatever this evil commanded.

The air was thick and pungent; the surrounding population were at this time oblivious to what had just been unleashed. Hanging there like a thick cloud of concentrated blackness it slightly condense and started to shrink, it was going down into a nothing just a whisper of its self. But the power did not diminish the evil did not shrink; it was disguising its self into something of nothing to be seen by the human eye. It was hiding in plain sight and soon it would be on its way. Searching for what it came for and using who and whatever it needed to achieve what it wanted. The blackness had almost gone the evil here hard to see but it was moving and moving away across the land. Unnoticed it would only be felt by its enemy and the souls it used controlling the bad and evil in certain people, otherwise no one would know it was there, that is even existed.

Life in the town carried on has it had done for countless years not many people were about not many cars on the roads. The evil moved unnoticed across the town like an invisible cloud. Most people were completely oblivious to it, but some, were not. They didn't know why but they got a shiver as if something had walked over their grave. They felt a little weird just for a moment. These people were bad; they had an evil streak in them. This is what was touched this is what was alerted as the darkness passed by them. If it needed it would use this to its advantage and when it needed it would rise these people up and make them do whatever it willed them to do.

They would not question it and they could not fight it, or even be able to explain it, they would just blindly do its will and have no explanation afterwards why they did what they did. The good and honest people were not affected and could not be controlled they were totally unaware of its presence or existence. Moving quickly the darkness rose high up in the sky and moved away from this place and headed off searching for what it had come to hunt down.

CHAPTER FOUR

Richard had got out of bed and gone to the toilet, he quietly let Max out the door the dog headed off to mark his spot and do what dogs do. He gave him a few minutes and turned back to look at Stephanie asleep in the bed, she looked peaceful and he was so glad she was very tough. Most people would of collapsed under this pressure and be torn apart mentally with what she had been through. But she seemed to be fighting back and being strong. She gave him Max? He had to smile slightly and took a deep breath letting it back out slowly. She needed him, and he would do all he could to save her and give her whatever she required. He noticed movement and turned to look outside, it was Max trotting back. He stroked and hugged him then closed and locked the door placing the two small wedges back under it. Max had a drink of water from the bowl Richard had placed on the floor for him then he settled back down and watched Richard get slowly and quietly back into bed. He settled and Stephanie moved and turned to face him. She opened her eyes and could just make out in the dark him looking down at her. The outside light shone in slightly and the small night light by the toilet gave her enough illumination to make his face out.

"Everything alright?" she asked still half asleep.

“Yes Max just needed to go out and do his business, go back to sleep all is secured” he said to her and smiled and she smiled up at him.

“You amaze me, you really do. I always knew you were special and you had a road to walk

You are one of a kind and I am so glad I had the time I did with you as children and I am so glad we are here now together” she moved and snuggled into him smiling as she did.

Putting his arm around her he pulled her close. She felt warm and he liked the feeling. They both lay there and had their own thoughts but were thinking about the same thing. The time when they were kids the time before this time of unrest and uncertainty, it was a good time and a happy time, it made both of them happy thinking about it. Stephanie fell back asleep and Richard tried to do the same but he didn’t sleep much more that night he was awake and keeping alert but was also bothered, and troubled, he had thoughts he was keeping to himself and feelings he was hiding, did he really believe all this?

The morning broke and Stephanie opened her eyes, she noticed she was in the bed alone and she sat up startled for a moment, but then settled back down when she saw Max sat at the bottom of the bed looking at her. She could hear Richard in the bathroom and watched the doorway for him to come out. He appeared and she smiled at him as he stood tall and scratching his backside. He had only some loose bottoms on and he glanced over at her as she looked at him.

"Good Morning" She said with a smile.

"Morning, how are you feeling, hope you had a good rest?" he said coming and sitting on the bed next to her.

"I needed it thank you"

"I am a little confused lass" He said with a slight frown as he looked down at her.

"Just, a little confused?" She asked with a straight and expressionless face.

"Well I never really knew or understood where you went, what you became, you told me your mother was some sort of witch?

"That is not the word I would use but if it helps you understand then yes, she was a powerful woman and was in touch with the ancient ways, she was a good woman, like your mother, she always said your mother was an angel and she would know"

He said nothing and his confused face had not changed. He was no wiser now then he was when he asked the question. He looked into her eyes for a moment then decided to leave it for another time.

"Do you want breakfast?" he asked

"I am very hungry yes please"

“They do full English here which is acceptable”

“I will try it, are you ok you seem distant” she said suddenly seeing Richard’s blank expression.

“I am fine, you get yourself up and ready and we shall go and sample it” he smiled and stood up and went back into the bathroom. She didn’t take her gaze from the doorway for a few moments then she glanced down at Max.

Richard was brushing his teeth and alone with his thoughts, he always trusted his gut instinct but this time he hoped he was wrong. This time he just hoped it was a time when his feelings were misguided. Something was not right here, something did not read correct. He just could not put his finger on it but the awkward void of mistrust and uncertainty had crept in without any warning or invitation. He took a mouthful of water and rinsed his mouth out. Looking at himself for a moment in the mirror he gazed into his own blue eyes. He sighed and shook his head looking down into the sink for a moment then back at himself in the mirror. He had become calmer and less volatile but sometimes that was the best way to be. He decided to carry on a little longer, play the game along for a while. Turning he walked back into the room, Stephanie was sat on the edge of the bed stroking Max and she looked up at him when he entered.

“All yours lass he said smiling a false smile.

“Thank you” she said knowing instantly something was wrong. She brushed past him and closed the door. Max came over and looked up at his master. Kneeling down Richard stroked his dog and looked into its eyes.

“I know mate, I know something is not right” Max returned the stare and didn’t move, standing back up he got dressed and checked out of the window. He took the two small wedges from under the door and put them back into his bag. He began to pack and got ready to leave but to where he didn’t know yet. He heard the bathroom door open and Stephanie came out she got dressed in the jogging pants and tee shirt Richard had supplied for her silently and saying nothing.

“First thing we have to get you some clothes and footwear, what else do you need, toiletries or whatever?” Richard asked her as she stood in front of him looking back at him. She seemed a lot better and more composed he could see the doubt and worry in her eyes. She gave a weak smile saying quietly.

“What is wrong, I can see something is bothering you?”

He looked at her for a moment not saying anything; he then took a breath in and let it out slowly, not taking his eyes from hers.

“Something is not making sense to me” He told her calmly

“None of it makes much sense, what are you saying if you want me to leave...?”

“See, there, that is so out of character of the Stephanie I knew” He tensed up slightly and Max walked by his side in a protective gesture.

“I am sorry, but I have been through so much, I have been ripped inside out and no, you are right, I am not the same character I was.” she touched her short cut hair and suddenly felt vulnerable and ashamed of how she must look to him.

“Aye I know lass, well let’s get going, in fact where the hell are we going?” he dismissed the other thoughts for another time, keeping them to himself for the moment, but he would not be letting his guard down and he was pleased Max felt it as well.

“I don’t really know, what we need to fight pure evil, pure good and where do we find that, I have no power of my own” she sat on the bed dejected and saddened once again. She put her head in her hands and sighed out painfully with emotion and anguish and started to sob.

“Don’t worry Stephanie we will get through it and we will win this thing, just try and stay strong for me and try to get your willpower and strength back” was all Richard could find to say, he should have sat next to her and hugged her but something, he did not know what, stopped him for doing it. She looked up at him and nodded, her eyes were red and she looked weak, standing again she collected herself and took a deep breath.

“Thank you, but please never hold anything back from me, I know you very well, more than you know Richard and I know when something is on your mind, I get that feeling right now”

“We can’t always trust our feelings now can we but, don’t worry, if I have anything to say at anytime I will say it” his face looked friendly again and it made her feel better instantly.

“You mentioned something about breakfast?” she asked him trying to smile through the heavy burden she was feeling.

“Well we need to get you a jacket and something for your feet” he said looking down at this bare footed woman in a tight tee shirt and baggy bottoms.

“I must look a right state I am sorry” she said becoming ashamed with her appearance

“Don’t be silly I am used to you looking like a shabby thing, you always did when you were ten, hair all over the place, scuffed shoes, dirty face”

“I was not, I was a clean and angelic little child” she defended seeing his face break into a smile and she welcomed it.

“You were rough as a dogs arse, we used to climb trees and have mud fights and you threw me into the tarn once”

“I did, didn’t I?” she smiled at the thought of their childhood antics.

“Things not changed that much, amazing how I dreamed of you saw you as you are now” he stopped talking and thought about it for a moment, thought actually how weird and strange that was. How the hell would he know what she looked like now as a grown woman? She saw him thinking and stood up and looked at him.

“You haven’t changed a bit” she said

“Not even a little bit? Some things are bigger now”

She clicked her tongue and smiled it felt good to smile and just for a moment feel good.

CHAPTER FIVE

Sheila had been abused all her life, first by her father and now by her husband. She had taken so much and been beaten down that many times she had no fight left in her. She knew she was not a perfect person she knew she had to be stronger but she could not. She was good and caring to her core. That's her problem everyone told her, you are too nice, too trusting. But she cannot help it, it is the way she is it's in her makeup. Only twenty eight but she looks ten years older sat on the chair sobbing. Her knees lifted up to her chest and she had her arms clasped around them. Looking dishevelled and weak scared and alone she knew her mental state could not take much more. It had been a particularly bad day; her abusive husband was in a very bad mood he always is when his football team loses. Today was no exception he had already hit her once earlier and she was still shaking from the impact of it. Their young daughter, Jayne, had annoyed him, she was doing nothing wrong but it didn't take anything to annoy him anyway. She knew he had dragged Jayne out into the garden for some reason. The child was just asking for some rabbit food for her beloved bunny in the wooden hutch at the bottom of the garden. He had gone mad at Jayne and screamed at her that loud it shook the child to the core.

That is when he hit Sheila for "interfering" which made Jayne cry as well.

"I am sick and tired of that fucking rabbit, it costs too much money and I am sick of feeding the fucking thing, it is going to feed us today" he had yelled at and pulled the horrified girl from the kitchen and dragged her screaming down to the hutch at the bottom of the garden. Jayne was shaking and pleading with her daddy. She watched in horror as he kicked open the hutch and dragged the rabbit from it; he smashed the defenceless animals head violently several times on top of the wooded hutch. It was limp and dead in his hands, thrusting it out towards his traumatised little girl her yelled.

"Go and give that to your mother we are having rabbit stew for tea"

"No, please no" she cried with so much sorrow it made her feel sick and weak, looking down at her dead pet in his hands. He violently took her hand and put the dead rabbit in it, he slapped her across the face and told her to get going and pointed to the kitchen door. She shook her head and cried uncontrollably and dashed off in fear and dread to the kitchen. He kicked the wooden hutch over and kicked it again cursing his anger out as he did.

The darkness was near it was like homing in on him, he had no idea he was not aware of a thing. But the darkness soon was in control of him and he would never understand how or what it would do and control him. He was bad, he had evil already in him and this is what gave the darkness power over him and over anyone like him.

Sheila did what she could to calm her distraught child, but there was not much she could do. Holding her poor daughter in her arms she felt the hurt, the pain and the anguish she was feeling. She hated herself for not being stronger but she just could not fight anymore. There was nothing left they both sobbed and felt the sadness deep within them.

Jayne looked up in fear as the door was opened and in walked her father; she pulled away and ran off out of the kitchen and up to her room.

"Cook that fucking thing now" He demanded to Sheila pointing to the dead rabbit on the kitchen floor where Jayne had dropped it.

"I don't know how too?" she said picking the rabbit up from the floor and looking over to him, just in time to see his fist smash into her eye, she staggered back and yelled out in pain.

"Fucking learn then, you stupid useless bitch" he shouted at her and casually walked into the living room and switched on the TV sitting in front of it saying nothing.

Sheila took deep breaths and held her throbbing eye, she shook her head and set about making a stew, she knew how wrong and sick this was but she could do nothing about it. She had to try and skin the rabbit and cook it but she had no idea how to do it. Knowing she had no choice knowing she could not say or ask him anything for fear of a beating she set about doing what she could and just hoped it was good enough for him.

He sat in silence and looked at the TV screen but was not really seeing what the program was; he was unconcerned about his actions, about his traumatised child or beaten wife. He didn't care and never had, but also he had a new feeling right now. It felt good to him, it felt right even. He had not felt this before his actions were necessary he had thought in the past but now he had enjoyed it, got some pleasure from it, a slight smile came across his face and he felt good about himself.

It was silent and quiet except for the TV program he was looking at and sat in front of, Sheila had done her best sobbing all the while but she had managed to put a meal together, it had broke her heart to cut up her daughters rabbit, her little pet but she knew she had to do it she had no choice. The stew was ready and she had laid the kitchen table. Shaking and breathing irregular she looked over to the cooker, it was time, the meal was ready. Fighting back her tears she started to put the vegetables out and lay the table. She knew how he liked it and always did it the way he wanted. The meat just looked like meat on a plate now, she had thrown the carcass away and cleaned up as she went along she could never leave a mess in the fear of a beating. Everything had to be just right all the time or she would pay the price. Her eye had swelled and it hurt but she fought to dismiss it and made sure everything was set out just right, just the way he like it, just the way it had to be.

Sheepish she walked into the living room and stood by the side of the settee submissively.

"About fucking time" he said glancing up at her with disgust.

"It's all ready" she said quietly.

"It better be good that is all I can say, go get her from up stairs it is time for her to eat" he said raising his voice that made her gasp and step back instinctively. Then she hurried off up stairs to try and persuade her daughter to come down for something to eat but dare not tell her what it was. Jayne was still sobbing on her bed, her thumb in her mouth and lay on her side. She looked up startled when her mother came in.

"Baby I need you to be strong OK, I need you to do as I say, please" Sheila said to her.

"No, mummy no I can't I hate him" she cried out again and Sheila took her in her arms and cried with her. Eventually pulling away she looked into her daughters teary eyes.

“Please baby, we just need to go eat some food then you can come back, I promise we will get away after this baby” her voice was quiet and weak and full of dread.

“You said that before and we are still here” Jayne said upset and scared.

“I know angle, I know but this time we will, I promise, please let’s just go have some food then we will talk more OK?”

Reluctantly they both slowly left the bed room both knowing they have no choice, Jayne was only young but she had learned quickly, learned not to disobey her father.

Silently they all sat at the kitchen table, no one moved until he was ready to eat, he looked over the spread in front of him. Making sure it was to his liking and as it should be. Each plate was in front with the food on; he always got the biggest portion and always was the one to start first. He took his knife and fork and took a taste of the meat. He chewed it and Sheila looked on in fear until her swallowed it, if he spat it out she was in trouble. He chewed slowly and then swallowed.

“It will do, I suppose” he said in an unimpressed way. Sheila started to slowly eat her meal but Jayne just stared at the meat on her plate, she knew it was her pet rabbit and she could not bring herself to eat it. He noticed and smiled he found it amusing and said to her.

"What's up doc" he laughed and looked over to Sheila expecting her to be laughing too.

"Please daddy" was all Jayne could say. It was all that was needed to trigger him off too.

"Eat you ungrateful little bitch, fucking it" he yelled at her making Sheila and Jayne shake and drop their knives and forks.

"Please daddy I am not hungry please" she pleaded with him tears rolling down her face.

Sheila reached over and tried to comfort her daughter but it was all the excuse he needed.

He violently erupted and it was to be a sad and devastating thing that he did.

The darkness within him took over and the evil that dwelled deep inside him implemented what he was about to do. He stood up lifting the table with him and threw it across the room. The rage within him was out of control and he had no power to stop it. Jayne screamed and fell back in her chair crashing to the floor; he took the knife in his hand and held it up high over her head, madness in his eyes and his face contorted with hatred.

"NO" Sheila screamed and dashed forward in her daughters defence. But she was no match for him, the knife was thrust at her and it cut her deep across the face, he then kicked her savagely across the room. She went flying back crashing into the cooker and collapsing to the floor. With super human strength and over whelming fear she somehow got to her feet and ran towards him before he could bring the knife down towards her daughter. She rammed into him and knocked him back. They both rolled onto the floor and across the kitchen. The knife was plunged deep into Sheila's back but the adrenaline was pumping through her veins and she had found some strength, from where she didn't know but she had found it. Punching and scratching at his face she pounded with all her might, she was possessed with anger, fear and the instinct to protect her child. She had poked him in the right eye blinding him as she did and scratched at his other eye. He pushed her off and rolled away temporally blinded in his other eye and hitting out wildly. She staggered to her feet and the knife was still in her back but she didn't feel it, the adrenaline was still strong and she had to escape, this was her only and last chance. She was bleeding and unsteady but she looked over for her daughter who had curled up in the corner petrified and unable to move.

He cried out in anger and got to his feet, he searched around the kitchen his vision impaired but he could still make out shapes with one eye. He lunged forward and grabbed at Sheila he started to punch at her head and scream out as he did. She felt the vicious blows and they dazed her. Frantically she fought him off but fell over as she did and the knife made its self felt as she knocked it painfully to the side. Reaching out she picked up the large pan on the floor she had cooked the vegetables in and lashed out as he came lunging forward once again. She hit him hard across the head with it, making a dull sickening sound as she did. Feeling frail she looked up saw him stagger back and fall over. She tried to stand but could not, the blood was covering her back and she was weak, she could feel the strength draining from her, looking to her daughter with tears in her eyes she screamed.

"Jayne, Run, get out run to the police, RUN" she desperately needed her daughter to escape to get away. She shouted again at her and the second time something in Jayne seemed to stir and as if she was in a daze she stood up and ran from the kitchen and out the house. Sheila was glad and tried to stand she was unsteady and weakening by the moment.

Positioning herself in the door way she stood unsteady and faced her husband who was now standing blood coming from the gash on the side of his head where she had hit him with the metal pan, he looked at her and snarled spitting blood from his mouth onto the floor.

"I am going to fucking kill you and that little bitch" he said with evil in his eyes.

It was all she had to hear she knew he meant it and she knew her life ended here, but she was not going to let him hurt her little girl anymore. She timed it good and when he lunged forward she hit him hard again across the face with the pan. Knocking him down she fell on top of him unable to stand anymore. Then with the last bit of energy and strength she had she repeatedly hit him and smashed his head to a pulp with the metal pan. When she could lift the pan no more she collapsed and felt the life drain away from her. Blood for both of them staining the kitchen floor as they both lay dead. No one would really know what caused all this to come about. Self defence would be the verdict no doubt and it would be the truth, not only defence for Sheila but for her child. People knew she had been abused and she had had enough on this day. But the real truth, the real reason was still there, the evil was still there in many people and the darkness would always find it and use it. The darkness moved on and headed to where it needed to go, awakening the evil of everything it touched and came into contact with. All controlling and all powerful it had an army at its disposal and they didn't know it yet.

CHAPTER SIX

After the breakfast that morning Richard had taken Stephanie to get some clothes and footwear from town then headed off again. She felt better in casuals and was comfortable. They were driving north something he always did when he was not sure where to go. It was like a default destination for him. Stephanie could tell something was on his mind she felt the slight chill from his attitude.

“Are you going to tell me what is on your mind?” she asked him not taking her eyes from the road ahead. He didn’t take his gaze away either when he answered.

“Nothing much, I am trying to figure out what the hell is wrong, and where the hell we are going, could you tell me where we are going Stephanie?” his tone was somewhat icy and she didn’t like it, she felt the coldness and abruptness in his voice.

“There is nothing wrong Richard it is has I have explained, no more, I mean you no harm and will do you no harm, I have a feeling you are beginning to mistrust me, or what I say, am I right?” she now turned her head and looked at him for the answer.

“I have been through a lot and I have seen too much, always followed my gut feeling and instinct; sometimes I bugger up and pay the price for it. But I do know things have changed and I have changed. I trust no one and it has always been that way. Now I see the impossible last night with that bloody Tower and you come screaming out" he slowed the Land Rover down and pulled to a stop by the side of the road and turned off the engine. For a moment Stephanie thought he was going to throw her out and drive off. But he turned in his seat and looked into her eyes. Waiting for an answer as he stared at her, she took a deep breath and let it back out quickly.

"There is something I never told you Richard, something from when we were together all them years ago, before any of this happened. Before we even realised anything like this could happen. But there was one person who told me one person who asked me to keep you safe. It was when we were only children but they knew even then, when we were still young and stupid, but this special person knew, they told me I would need to keep you safe one day, I didn't understand then obviously but I do now" she paused and looked at his unchanged expression but she knew him well enough to know his mind would be racing back and trying to remember and figure out who she meant. He slowly shook his head and she could see he was remembering and didn't want to remember, but had no choice right now

"No, don't even go there Stephanie" he said to her firmly but calmly.

"The only thing that can overcome this evil thing is pure good, something that is just as strong if not stronger than the evil but it's opposite not bad or evil but good and kind and pure. Something that is so strong and powerful the darkness has no chance of surviving it"

"Stop Stephanie stop now" Richard sat back in his seat and looked out of the window but was seeing nothing his mind was racing and his thoughts chasing his mind.

"Richard I am condemned to eternal pain and torture, but you must fight you must win this thing there is no hope for me, none, I am an empty vessel now. I am only here to save you and to show you what you must do, where you must go and who we must see, please Richard listen to me" she put her hand on his arm and he turned to look at her, she could see for the first time the hurt in his eyes. The memory that had put the hurt here still shocking him like a bolt of electricity going through his body and soul, it was the only thing that could do this to him, and she could feel his pain.

"Why have you come back, why did you tell me something different last night, you are beginning to contradict yourself Stephanie, something is very wrong here" he suddenly snapped out of his train of thought and became defensive towards her.

"Listen to me Richard, if my soul my life my very being is damned then so be it, but you must listen to me, I didn't know for sure I still don't I am confused as well but we have to try this and believe me there is nothing else, and I mean nothing else here or on the other side, no plain of existence can help you except this one thing Richard"

"You came back out of the darkness; you said you came back because..."

"I came back for you, this one promise I made to her Richard, the only true force that can beat this evil, this darkness and if you do not listen and do not comply you will be joining me I can assure you of that. You are not powerful enough to beat this one, no one is, the only thing that truly defeats evil is good. You need help, we need help and we need the divine help of a true celestial being, accept it or not we need the help of the one person who brought you into this world Richard, the most kindest and strongest and purest person you have even known, we need that one person Richard, we need your Mother" She watched him shake his head and not believe what she was saying, he knew Stephanie met his mother and he knew his mother liked Stephanie. But his childhood had been rough and ready and full of pain and fights and he had to constantly defend himself, but his mother was always there for him and always on his side. He looked over again to Stephanie and said nothing for a short time then he searched in her eyes and could see she was desperate for him to believe her and she kept looking at him in the same way knowing this was a pivotal moment in his whole dysfunctional life.

"My mother is dead Stephanie, you must know this, she never said anything to me, never knew what I was to become she just loved me unconditionally and there was no hint that she..."

"Richard she didn't know that is not the point, she knows now, she is watching you Richard, you have to believe this" Her voice became worried as she felt she was losing him, she didn't want him shutting this out. It was something he never talked about and never opened that door to that time. Shaking his head he looked away from her, glancing back over his shoulder he looked at Max who was asleep on the back seats.

"It was the saddest day of my life when I saw her take her last breath, I was there, something that was so strong so powerful suddenly gone, it was life changing for me" he said looking back at her and she was happy he had opened up and said this to her.

"I know I know it hurt you more than anything else, you loved your mother Richard and when your father passed years before you looked after her. She asked me to look after you when she was gone, she told me you were her whole world and she was so proud of you. She was a truly an extraordinary woman" Stephanie said in a sympathetic and convincingly low voice, wondering if he would ask how she knew.

"They just do not make them like her anymore Stephanie; she was one of a kind"

"Exactly this is exactly what I am trying to tell you. And you need her now Richard, we have to find someone who knew her, was close to her"

"I was close to her and knew her what are you talking about?" Richard said puzzled for a moment staring at her with a frown.

"She told me about some church she used to go too?"

"When, when did she tell you this, why have you not mentioned any of this before?"

"This is the time for it to be mentioned, I had no idea back then, no idea what she meant but she knew, she knew something was going to happen sometime in your life and that time is now, I only fully understand at this moment, she was the purest thing in your life. The one woman who protected you like no other, she gave you life and is the only person who can save your life, and now your very soul" she touched Richard's face with her hand and looked at his blue eyes, worried that he would reject all this and leave.

"I can't believe you have never mentioned any of this before, it doesn't make sense, how do I know you are who you say you are, something just is not right here" he suddenly became more defensive again and pulled away from her hand.

"I understand your concern, I never told you because there was never any reason or need too, but what I have now seen and have experienced the power and ferocity of this dark evil. Richard it all suddenly came back to me. The only thing the only chance we have is pure good, to beat pure evil. You need her and we need to find a way to find her, please believe me there is no other person or thing living or dead that can help or stop this, My mother was special and she knew your mother was special, it's something we can't comprehend".

"She died years ago, there is no way" he told her shaking his head.

"My mother died but I still could see her, all I know is it all came flooding back to me, and I had to get out and too you. I was confused scared and bewildered when you pulled me back. Only now is it all becoming clear. I was able to escape I was able to get you to get me out for a reason. There must be a reason, the only reason it can be is to get you to get the help from the only person who can help" she stopped and found it hard to make him understand and she was muddling her words and becoming confused herself, she wanted to grab him and shake him to make him understand.

Richard said nothing and started the vehicle back up; he slowly drove off and drove down the road. He was alone with his thoughts for a moment and Stephanie knew it best to leave him there. She looked back at Max who was still asleep and oblivious to everything that was going on right now. In a way she envied him for that, she could feel the lump in her throat. She suddenly came over very emotional and saddened. She held back the tears and turned away looking out of the side window at the passing scenery. Holding back her tears was not easy but she didn't want to break down at this moment and it took all her will power and strength to stay calm and composed.

"If it helps let the flood gates open Lass" Richard said not looking at her, he knew she was upset and knew it would help her to let the tears flood out.

"I will be fine" Stephanie said more in defiance than anything else. She had been scared and perplexed but suddenly knew now what she must do; it had all been hazy to her at first not really understanding until now. But she knew that the only person who can help who can defeat their foe was the one person Richard would never agree to put in any danger.

"I do not know if any of this is true or has you say, Even when we were kids I felt different with you Stephanie we have always had a special bond. I can see you now are struggling. I can understand your pain and frustration. But you must understand how all this sounds. You must understand how strange and just damn right impossible this situation seems and the answer to this situation from you is?" he glanced over to her for a long moment and then back on the road ahead.

"Yes I know it must sound very bizarre and you find it hard to accept and understand, it is not easy to explain and I wish I could do a better job of it"

"It just doesn't make sense to me; it has come out of the blue, out of nowhere, how can this suddenly be the answer?. Everything that has happened, this darkness the fucking tower your mother this evil thing, suddenly the answer is there all along, my mother?" he scoffed and shook his head clicking his tongue.

Stephanie didn't like the way he did it and knew she was fighting a losing battle.

She needed to try a different approach or she needed help, but whatever she needed she could do with it quickly and just hoped something or someone could provide it.

"I am sorry you don't believe me Richard, I am so sorry for my inadequacy but I am trying very hard to explain something I don't fully understand myself"

"Well I sure as hell don't understand it; we will meet whatever is coming head on"

“It is not what is coming, it is what it controls you can’t just fight everyone and everything Richard, it controls evil it controls whatever is bad. Everyone and everything is a potential threat a foe what if a mob of twenty men come for us, then what?” she knew she had to be callous and to the point to get through his stubbornness.

“I will fight, I am not going to ask my mum for help” he said it in a sarcastic way that Stephanie resented he shook his head and didn’t want to talk about it anymore.

“You are being pig headed and unreasonable, your stubbornness will not win this one, I know what your mother told me, I know she is the key to this and the sooner you get off your fucking high horse and admit it the better” Glaring at him she waited for his answer, he didn’t look at her and was quiet for a few moments then he shot her a stare.

“I will sort it out when the time comes” he said calmly.

“It controls evil, it manipulates it is only a matter of time before it controls a bad police officer, we are arrested we are taken to the cells and no one will see us again Richard Cushing. You are not that stupid. You must understand you have no one helping you on this one” she could not really believe what she was hearing she knew he was not that stupid. But then something dawned on her. He was shielding, he didn’t trust what she was saying so there for didn't trust her. It was the vibe she had felt earlier from him, something was on his mind something was bothering him and that is why he was not cooperating with her explanation.

"No one helping me on this one eh?" he looked at her with cold eyes and then looked back forward to the road ahead.

"You know what I mean" she told him folding her arms across her chest and huffing out a long breath she was annoyed and frustrated and suddenly the fear of it all came flooding back to her. She could not talk anymore she could not make him believe. Holding herself together she fought the fear that rose within her. The only man on the planet who could help didn't believe or trust her; it was not an ideal situation to be in.

Max stirred on the back seat and Richard noticed it, he looked for somewhere to stop and let the large dog out to stretch his legs.

Stephanie was quiet and fighting the hurt inside, she could not talk anymore at the moment and although he was cold towards her she didn't resent him for it.

Knowing his caution was a safety mechanism she let him go his own way for a while until she could think of something to convince him otherwise.

Slowing down he stopped the Land Rover and checked all around the road, he then got out and let Max out of the back. The dog stretched his long powerful body and yawned. He shook himself and trotted off to the grass verge by the side of the road and did what dogs do. Richard opened the back and got some water and poured it into a bowl for his dog when he returned. Looking up and down the road keeping watch he waited for his dog to finish and take a drink. Breaking a pack of dog meat in two he fed Max and they were soon back in the vehicle and heading up the road again.

Eventually Richard broke the silence and spoke but without looking at Stephanie.

"If what you say is true and we need this help, how is it supposed to materialise? What the hell is supposed to happen?"

"I don't know, I do not have all the answers I am only telling you, trying to tell you what I know, what is the only thing that can defeat this power this force coming for us like I said I do not have all the answers, I understand your caution but you are playing a very dangerous game by just dismissing this as another adversary you can fight and win, I know what I saw, experienced and it is not something I ever want to do again" she looked back at him and kept doing so until he turned his head to return her gaze.

"Alright Lass let's say I believe you, I can't just fight this, but I do not understand what all this about my mother is. It is just too farfetched for me to comprehend. I can't just sit here and think after all this time..." he stopped when he noticed a police car in his rear view mirror. He kept an eye on it and checked his speed, he was not breaking any law but he still slowed slightly. Stephanie became scared when he suddenly stopped talking and checked his mirror, seeing his narrowing eyes and caution.

"What is it?" she asked nervously.

"Coppers behind us, probably nothing we are doing nothing wrong"

"Oh no, do you think?" she asked looking forward and dare not look back out of the window

"Calm down we are ok, nothing we can't handle"

"How long have they been there?"

"Just pulled up but very quickly, they keeping a steady pace and distance now"

"What do you want me to do?" she said trying to control her breathing.

"Stay bloody calm for a start if we are stopped don't say anything unless asked and do not act nervous. We have done nothing wrong after all"

He watched as the blue lights were turned on and the police car sped up, the siren was loud and made Stephanie miss a breath the car raced up and then around the Land Rover. Richard watched as it sped away and down the road. He stayed at the same speed and could see quite a way ahead on the open road the police car had raced on and was almost out of sight now. He sighed and looked over at Stephanie who was already looking back at him.

"Where are we going?" she asked him

"Somewhere I have not been enough and somewhere very special, we are going back in time Stephanie going to remember another period and hope to get some answers, or at least some vibrations or at least bloody something"

"Good, we need to do bloody something that is for sure" she said settling back down in her seat and folding her arms across her chest she just looked forward and said no more.

Richard paid her no more attention he had other things on his mind, things from his past. Things that he had not, remembered for many years. But now suddenly something was drawing him back there and he felt compelled to follow the feeling. It was going to be an emotional journey but it had to be done. He was not totally convinced she was right but he had to at least try he knew this. Locking away his youth behind this mental door and never opening it was what he had always done. But now he had to throw that door open and remember and see what lay there. What forgotten thoughts and secrets could help if any? He drove and said nothing, he couldn't; he was too deeply within himself. He never spoke of his past to anyone, he kept it a secret and that is how it had always been. But Stephanie was part of that time. The only one who had met his mother and now it seemed she had been keeping this secret also. What was to come he didn't know but at least he needed to try and find out. Try and put some logic to it all, try and understand what needed to be done. It was such a strange and alien feeling to him to be doing this but he knew he had to get it straight in his head. Not a lot bothered him especially from his past but now the flood gates were to open and the force of the memory would be overwhelming. This whole situation would have been laughed away if someone told him about it two days ago, but now he was living it, a girl he had not seen for almost thirty years shows up, he witnesses some evil impossible happening and is now being told to go back to his roots where his mother told a ten year old girl all this was going happen. He thought it all madness. But then again seeing a fifty foot demolished stone tower rebuild in front of his eyes then disappear into the ground again was just as mad. The girl who was his best friend when he was ten years old suddenly appears after all these years and tells him a bizarre and wonderful story about some evil presence is even weirder.

He didn't know what the hell he had got himself into but he would soldier on like he has all his life and take what comes, it was how he lived and it had stood him in good stead so far.

CHAPTER SEVEN

The train was fast and it always raced past this cemetery at high speed, the school kids often came down to watch it, and some like these three sometimes put their old pennies on the track, waiting for the train to come and ride over them. School had just finished and the three boys ran down to the track they knew the train would be due any minute. Racing through and jumping over the grave stones of the cemetery they headed over the pathway and down the small embankment to the railway line. One of the boys the smallest went to the line and put his ear to it. He could feel and hear the vibration of the train on the track some distance away. The second boy took his old fashioned large penny from his side pocket and carefully laid in on the shiny metal track. They all then backed up and waited. A few minutes later the railway track began to quietly sing, a low hum then a more prominent vibration could be heard.

"It's here" the small boy shouted with enthusiasm. They all stood and the speeding train raced past them. The carriages racing past in an almost blur they all watched and stood still the wind from the train almost blowing them over at one point then suddenly as fast as it came the train was gone. Heading off away down the line and getting smaller into the distance they all peered after it and then looked at each other.

"Where did it go did you see it?" the second boy said searching around for the coin.

"It's here" The middle of the boys said as he picked the coin up and looked at it flattened to two times it original size it was thin and markings could still be seen.

"Let's have a look the smallest boy said coming over to inspect the coin.

"Shit run, its Bentley" The tallest boy said in panic has he saw two larger boys walking fast towards them. Scowling and looking angry, then they both broke into a run. Only the middle sized boy stood and didn't move or run away. He stood solid and put the penny in his pocket. The two larger boys got to him and stopped they looked at the other two running off and away but didn't chase them they turned and stood around the remaining boy.

"What you doing here Cushing, this is our place not yours, we have told you before" Bentley said in a threatening manner, his face up close to Richard's.

The two boys were bigger and older than him, but he didn't seem fazed by it, he seemed calm and just stared back at the boys staring at him.

“This is a free place, no one can tell anyone not to come here” Richard said.

“Oh no shit head, this is our turf, and no one, I mean no bugger comes here except us and the ones we say can, you are going to have to be taught a lesson”

“You are going to get hurt you little fucker” The other boy said and that was the trigger that set the fight in motion. Three of them set about each other and no one was to see it happen.

“Richard my son you have been fighting again?” His mother said as he walked into the house, she had seen him coming down the pathway to the front door from the window.

A small woman, with short greying hair and simple clothes she stood waiting for him in the hallway. He stopped and looked at her, his face cut and bruised and his shirt torn, the black dirty marks on his school blazer evident where he had been rolling about and fighting on the ground in the dirt and muck.

“They were wankers mum” was his defence pure and simple it was his only explanation.

“The world is full of them you can’t fight them all son you are only twelve years old come on let’s have a look at you”

They both went into the kitchen and he took off his jacket and torn shirt. He had scuff marks and grazes on his shoulders and arms. His mother told him to sit and she got the first aid box from the cupboard. Sitting next to him she began to clean his wounds. Sitting in silence he let his mother do what she has always done and look after him.

"Sorry mum" he finally said looking at her kind and loving face.

"You do not have to fight everyone, no matter what your father says"

"Self defence this time mum they started it"

"So you just had to finish it eh?"

"There was nowhere to run; honest I didn't have a choice"

"Well I believe you but please remember that not every action demands a reaction, sometime on action is the strongest reaction"

"Whatever you say mum" he smiled at her as she shook her head and smiled back at him, she cleaned off the blood and wiped away the dirt, he didn't once complain.

"So what was it about this time?"

"Two wankers started it bloody Bentley and his gay friends"

"Started what, why were you fighting?"

"They said I was on their turf and didn't have permission to be there so I had to be hurt"

"Oh for pity's sake turf you say where is this?" she shook her head in disbelief.

"Just some place" he said sheepishly.

“Where Richard Cushing” she demanded looking at him in the eye.

“Railway line by the cemetery” he said taking a breath knowing he was not suppose to be there and she would probably scold him now. She stopped what she was doing and calmly looked at him then said.

“Did I not tell you it is dangerous to play by them railway lines, so why did you still go down there, why did you go against my wishes?”

“Sorry mum” was all he said but knew it was way inadequate for a justification

“Not enough, I want an explanation”

“Because I am an idiot and should listen to you because you know best mum, I am sorry and will not go down there again” he said almost like a recital.

“Don’t you try and patronise me you little shit” she said half joking.

“Never mum, I know better”

“Why did you go down there, what did you do?” she asked and carried on cleaning his last cut on his forehead.

Taking the flattened penny from his pocket he showed her it with a smile and proud look on his face. She took it and inspected it and then gave him it back, he replaced it in his pocket.

"So what are you going to do with that, it is now worthless and no use to anyone, was that worth the beating you took here do you think?" she asked looking up at him as she put the first aid box together again and shut it.

"But I can't just back down mum?" he said a little confused.

"Why can you not just walk away, why can you not just let the words ride over your head and just walk away, you cannot fight everyone my boy" she implored

"I had no choice, I had nowhere to run, I am not just letting them kick the shit out of me ma, what am I suppose to do?" he said frustrated and perplexed

"Yes if your back is up against the wall and you have nowhere to go or a way out fair enough. But if you can walk away, if you can avoid confrontation then why not do it, I know your father tells you to hit first and not stop until you have won, I hear him talking to you, giving you all this advice but sometimes turning the other cheek means more and makes you a bigger man" she smiled at him knowing his young active mind didn't really understand what she was telling him.

"I don't know ma, is it not a sign of weakness running away letting them walk all over you, being bullied, I am not letting no one bully me, I do not go looking for trouble it just seems to come and find me. Anyway Bloody Bentley had it coming"

"I do not expect or want you to be bullied, I want you to stick up for yourself but you always get into these situations son, you just don't seem to be able to walk away from anything. Just promise me you will try to walk away from trouble when you can, please?"

"I will try mum, just for you I will try, thank you that sounded like an old country and western song actually" he said smiling at her.

"Cheeky sod, I will always be here for you, always, you never forget that, just ask for me and I will be there, we are all heading for a better place and there we will never need to fight again, just have some faith and all will be at peace you will see, I will always be there"

"Whatever you say ma, whatever you say" he smiled and gave her a hug which she welcomed and enjoyed immensely.

"You are a good lad Richard you just need some guidance and some grounding"

"I will have you to guide me and ground me so I am fine" he smiled at her cheekily

"Whatever you say, now bugger off and get changed, your dad will be home soon and I have not started tea yet" She pushed him away and he smiled at her. Standing he saw her take the small silver crucifix from around her neck she kissed it and said something under her breath then tucked it back away under her blouse again.

Walking up the stairs to his bedroom he took the penny from his pocket and looked at it again, he stopped and thought about what his mother had said to him, was it worth the effort.

He liked it and it was unique he thought, they had tried before but the penny flew off and they never found it so he was glad about finding this one. Yeah it was worth it, he had won the fight the two others were left laying there and he walked home so yeah, he was proud of this time, he carried on up to his room and closed the door.

That evening after dinner Richard had to help wash the dishes at his Father's order come request. Later he sat down across from his dad who wanted to ask him something. A small but strong man, his father stood no messing from anyone, he had been brought up the old fashioned Yorkshire way, fight or flight you stuck up for yourself or be beaten down.

"Your mother tells me you came home battered again?" He said sat in his chair looking over at Richard who had just finished the dishes and had come back into the living room.

"Yeah, they were wankers' dad" he said as the two of them started their conversation his mother had gone up stairs for a bath.

“How many how big what was it about?” his dad asked in a straight forward way.

“Bigger than me a year up, two of them and they said I should not be where I was without their permission, it was their turf” was his explanation once again.

“Aye, well did you belt em hard and get in first?”

“Yes, I hit them and kept hitting them until they could not hit me dad”

“Good lad, nah then never let anyone bully thy, they are cowards, bloody cowards does yer hear me, you have to show em who is the boss lad”

“I did dad I did, they were left on the floor I walked away”

“Reet listen, I need help next week, you can come and work with me, so next week you go sick from school, I will get tha mother to write a note for tha”

“Ok dad, great doing a roofing job are we?”

“Aye and it won’t be easy so make ready lad”

“Brilliant” Ray smiled and knew he was in for a little money when the job was finished.

“It’s gonna be a reet bugger in fact, but it will put you some brass in yer pocket lad”

“I am ready and brass is always good in my pocket dad” he smiled and knew it was going to be hard work but he didn’t mind, it always felt good helping his dad on jobs and getting out of school, on top of that he got paid for it. He had been working with his dad before and always had good respect for him, seeing how hard his father worked and how strong he was for a small man. Richard looked up to him and knew he was of old stock, old school he loved both his parents and considered himself a lucky lad in that respect.

CHAPTER EIGHT

Richard stopped the Land Rover at the top of the road, he looked down to the cemetery below, the same one he use to play in when he was a child, with the same railway line that ran down at the bottom. He was lost for a moment in his thoughts; he then opened the door and got out. Stephanie did the same and could see he was in another place; his memories had taken over his mind for a moment. Stephanie opened the back door and let Max out to stretch his legs and sniff about. It was a dull day and clouds were covering the sky. Looking around Stephanie shivered with the cold that suddenly she felt in the air. She knew not to disturb him at this time and let him wonder off down the pebbled pathway. She stood by the Land Rover and watched. Max came back and was going to follow his master but also seemed to know not to at this moment and he sat and looked on but not letting Richard out of his sight. The place was old but well kept some gravestones had fresh flowers there that had been left recently. It was still a place people visited but a place He had not been too since his mother had died. He walked down the pathway and across the small grass area. The railway line had been fenced across now. You could not get near the lines like you could when he was a child. He thought to himself that the kids of today were not like they were when he was younger, a fence was not even thought of back then, kids knew better. He sighed out and shook his head and turned to face the gravestone that he was next too.

Stephanie could see him from the top of the hill and the side of the road she watched him as he stood silent and looked down at a grave stone she knew whose it would have been, Max was watching his master intensely but not moving. The rest of the cemetery seemed deserted and quiet and it was welcomed by Richard. He looked down at the grave stone with the inscription of Geoff Cushing and Margaret Cushing. The grave of his parents he was lost in silence and in thought as he looked at the fading head stone. Only being awoke from it as a train raced past him on the other side of the steel railings. It was going fast and he looked up at it as it sped past. He turned and looked back and then saw the small weak looking man looking at him. They locked eyes for a moment, the man was only small and looked very old, he was stood by the side of the grave of his parents but Richard felt no menace no evil from him. Looking into the gaunt face this man reminded him of someone, then he thought harder and smiled, yes, he looked like the actor Anthony Hopkins.

“Hello” was all Richard said to him

“Hello, it has been a very long time?” the man said in a voice that matched his frail look.

"Have we ever met?" Richard asked calmly

"No but I do know who you are, and I am glad you have finally come here"

"Who are you?" he said looking back at his parent's grave.

"I look after the cemeteries residents shall we say" he smiled slightly not taking his eyes off Richard for a moment as he spoke.

"Do you now, well that must be a quiet job" looked back at him and knew this man was of another time, another world or dimension. He felt no animosity or evil at all but he was curious at who this man was.

"It is more hectic than you could imagine, people die with worry and ideas and thoughts and unanswered questions. Things that never got said, warnings they need to relay it is a very busy and very hectic believe it or not" he was dressed in very old fashioned clothing and slightly hunched over somewhat.

"That is what you do is it?" Richard said unaffected by what he was hearing and seeing.

"Something, like that but there are only certain people who can understand it and see it, only the ones who have to be told something or need something from here"

"You say you know who I am?" Turning his full attention to the little man and looked him straight in the eye and was stood solid in stance and expression.

“You are Richard Cushing, ” the man said expressionlessly.

“I am stood by a grave stone named Cushing that is not hard to figure out is it, you have to do better than that old man” he told him.

“You need the help from the only person who can help, you are long overdue here, late in your arrival but you are here now and it is very good that you are”

Looking back down to the grave stone and reading his mother’s name then his father’s name in his head, sighing out he looked back to the intense stare of the old man looking at him.

“My mother is that what you are saying to me?”

“Of course, we have been waiting for you; she has been waiting for you Richard”

“Why now, after all what I have been through why is she there now?”

“She has always been there, always been with you, you just need to call to her, you never asked. You need to ask and call to her speak her name invite her back and she will help you”

“Why should I believe you I have never seen or met you before?”

“There is always a better place, somewhere you can be free and no more fighting your mother is the purist and strongest woman I have ever known. Her power is intense and she is amazingly powerful. You ask her to help you, you need to ask her, call her to your side and she will be there it is only you who can do this"

"Hmmm" Richard shook his head slowly not really knowing what to believe.

The man took something slowly out of his pocket and placed it on the grave stone of Richard's parents. He looked again at Richard and said once more.

"Call to her and she will help"

Reaching down Richard took the small silver crucifix from the headstone; looking at it he instantly recognised it as his mothers.

"She was buried with this how did you get it?" He said sharply looking up but the man was gone. He looked around for him but there was no sign.

"Speak her name Richard, she will come" the voice was in the air but he did not know where it came from. He held the cross in his hand and knelt down by the grave.

"Mother, Father I am sorry for what I have become and sorry I put you through what I did. I miss you both terribly and never loved anyone as much. Please forgive me and know I miss you both with all my heart. I have been lost but now I believe I am found and have come back, I owe you both so much and wish I had done so much more for you" he bowed his head and was silent and in thought for some time before he stood and walked back up towards Max who greeted him and then they went to stand by the Land Rover. Stephanie came close to him and could see his disturbed and strange look.

"Are you alright, is that their grave down there?" she said knowing it was a stupid question as soon as she said it.

"Yes it is, the old man, he gave me this" Richard opened his hand and showed her the crucifix"

"Old man what old man?" Stephanie asked looking at the silver crucifix in his hand.

"The one down there by the graveside, he said if I call my mother she will come and be there, he gave me this it is her crucifix, she was buried with this Stephanie"

"Richard you were alone the whole time, there was no one else there, I watched you the whole time you were talking to the gravestone" she said confused.

"There was a old man he was dressed like from another century he was talking to me stood next to me, he gave me this crucifix" he insisted then calmed and realised. Looking back down he scanned the whole place and it was empty there was no one else there except them.

Max sat next to his Masters leg; he looked down at the cemetery and was silent and still, he seemed to be looking at something but it was not evil in any way he just stared.

"Are you alright?" Stephanie asked looking at Richard then down into the cemetery area then back at Richard again with concern.

"The trouble is you are too busy growing up and taking people for granted, you don't realise they are growing old watching your back all this time. Not until it is too late do you realise what they have given up for you, sacrificed from their own life to give to your life"

"Can I go down there and pay my respects?" Stephanie asked him. He just nodded and then got back into the Land Rover followed by Max. Stephanie had never witnessed him like this before and she quietly walked down the pathway to the head stone. She looked at it for a short while and then knelt down saying softly.

"I only met you a couple of times, you once said to me to look after your son when you are gone; I tried and will continue to do so but I am confused what to do now?" she sighed and looked at the weathered stone in front of her. She felt nothing and could sense nothing. She jumped back as a train sped past on the lines behind her the force of the wind making her wince. She looked at it then looked back at the headstone for a moment.

"Please help me" she said then bowed her head for a moment before she walked back up to the Land Rover, she got in and looked at Richard who was deep in thought it seemed.

"When I was a kid we use to come here, play down there by the railway lines, there was no fence up then, it was just open. There was no need for a bloody fence. We were not that stupid to walk onto the lines when a train was coming, didn't have to be told of the obvious danger. No one to complain and shout about the safety of it all, we just played and fought and got on with it. If you did something wrong you got a clip around the ear hole and you learned a lesson and carried on, wiser. Today it is shite, soft and ridiculous, I have never understood it" he sighed out and shook his head then looked out the side window down towards the cemetery again his thoughts racing around with his memories.

"Times change Richard; we can do nothing about it"

"Change for the worse if you ask me" he then started the Land Rover back up and pulled away, Stephanie put her seat belt on and said nothing for a short while.

"What do we do now, where are we going who was the man talking to you?" she said quickly and fast like a machine gun.

"Go to a little church, you said something about a small church didn't you before?"

"Yes that's right, do you know which one it is?"

"I think so, she used to tell me when she was a child in care and looked after by nuns she used to go to a small church near by the home she was in?"

"Nuns, what do you mean?" Stephanie asked confused.

"My mother and all her siblings were put in a home when they were very young, their dad buggered off in the army and wanted no more to do with them. She was brought up there and it was run by nuns who looked after the children"

"I never knew that, what happened to your mother's mother?"

"She died after child birth of the youngest; mum was the eldest of the lot"

"I am sorry I didn't know that Richard, she must have had a hard life"

"Yes she did, they were very strict and hard on the kids in that home she got a job when she was sixteen, held down two jobs actually. When she was eighteen she left the place and finally had a little bit of a life"

"I remember seeing a photo of her on the wall of your house when she was younger she was a very beautiful woman" Stephanie said remembering with a smile.

"Inside and out yes" he said quietly and was alone again with his thoughts, Stephanie decided to say no more until he spoke again, she knew how difficult and confusing this was to him and didn't want to add to it in any way. She left him in his own world of remembrance and just looked out of the window. She knew the urgency of it all but also knew she would not be able to rush him into anything; he would have to kick into gear himself. She just hoped it would be very soon because she knew what was coming for them and it would be very close by now. She had done all she could and was happy at least he was now accepting what was happening. She wondered who the man was he said he was talking too, how he had got the crucifix and she wondered what would happen when the darkness was upon them. It made her shiver and swallow with dread. Folding her arms across her chest she looked out of the window at the passing Yorkshire scenery. She saw the stone buildings the fields beyond and could imagine a young Richard Cushing claiming it all. It made her smile, she actually smiled at the thought of him as a boy, knowing what he was like, a right tare away, but it had made him what he is today and many people had to be grateful for that. She remembered their time together how he was sometimes distant even then. But also loving he had a gentle side not many had every witnessed, a comedic side telling jokes. But all that seemed gone now hidden away under the hard tough adult exterior that was with him these days. Sighing inwardly she looked out of the front window at the road ahead the road they were travelling. Into the unknown and what was coming after them was never going to stop. There seemed no hope but she had to cling onto some kind of hope, and it kept her sane and kept her going. She knew he was the toughest and strongest child to man she had ever known, but this was a different strength he now needed. Not brute strength but inner emotional strength a power to take his past and make it work for him in the present, to take from behind to show his way forward. She was not sure what else she could do or how she could help him but she was going to try, try with every part of her being, it was the only chance she had, the only chance any of them had. Her thoughts drifted to when she was stood on the tower's ruins, she couldn't even remember how long ago it was now, she knew her mother's soul was down there she knew she had to try and get to her. She thought she had enough knowledge and enough power to do so but how wrong she was. She was sucked in and demolished she thought she could break the spell to release her mother's soul but all she did was release the dark evil it was encasing. The pain she felt the suffering she witnessed destroyed her and she closed her eyes thinking about it. Shaking it from her mind she opened her eyes and took in the countryside and just hoped Richard had grown into be the man she hoped he was.

CHAPTER NINE

The darkness was relentless not stopping just seemed to be drifting on its way knowing where to go, knowing it would get there homing in on its target. People were oblivious about it until it touched them. All controlling and all consuming it just was so concentrated evil it could manipulate evil and control evil where ever it found it. It can gather an army within no time just by being around bad and immoral people it will always have countless souls to command and they will be able to do nothing to stop it.

Jasmine was a black woman who was an angry soul; she always has had a temper and always wanted her own way. Today was no exception her husband was tired, he had left her over a year before and tried to start a new life away from her but she didn't let him be. He paid her money he helped her out on many occasions when he had no commitment to do so, they were legally separated but she would not let him get on with his life. Driving over to his house she was already in a rage. She drove unknowingly through the darkness and it touched her deeply within her black soul. Out of control now and nothing she could do nothing about it the evil within her was over powering and all consuming. Having no guilt or compassion just the hate that raged deep inside her. Strangely it made her feel good, strong and powerful, it made her brave and determined. The darkness had only touched her, but that is all that was needed it was like an ignition to her evil dark side. Moved on and heading away the darkness needed to do no more, it could stay and control her but it didn't have to. The evil inside her would do that. She gritted her teeth together and the anger rose like a bolt of electricity within her. Suddenly all the hate and resentment she had towards her husband multiplied tremendously. She put her foot down and headed to the small rented house much faster. Speeding along she had no regard for safety of others and never stopped at a zebra crossing almost hitting two school children as they were crossing. Running a red light she raced on and started to curse out in the car in a rage at everything and everyone around her. Almost losing control of the car she sped around the tight corner and down the narrow street. Screeching to a halt she opened the car door and slammed it shut with force. Striding quickly up to the front door she tried to go straight in but the door was locked. She cursed and started to hammer on the wooden door relentlessly. Dressed in an all in one long dress and her long hair tied back in a pony tail she belted the door as hard as she could. Swapping hands when her right fist became tired cursing out all the time she was pounding away.

The door was suddenly opened and a large African man stood there with anger in his eyes and distaste expression on his face towards her

"What the hell are you doing Jasmine?" he demanded.

"Fuck off" she said and forcefully pushed past him and into his house. He looked around and then up the road before closing it and heading back inside.

"I am not putting up with this shit, we are separated what the hell do you, want now?" he said looking at her looking back at him with hate in her eyes.

"I want what is right I am sick of all this crap, I want more money and I want what I am entitled too, so you just better cough up you big stupid Bastard" she yelled at him.

"You are not right in the head woman, you need help, you already have the house, the car and everything else we ever owned I walked away with nothing or have you forget this fact" he shouted back at her and came closer to her in the centre of the room, he was dressed smart in trousers and a dress shirt. She looked him up and down and then around the room.

"You look pathetic; you dress like a white gay man"

"I dress however I want to dress it is no concern of yours" he glared down at her as he stood a good six inches above her smaller frame.

"You seeing a white bitch I have been told?"

"It's none of your concern, who I am seeing?"

"Fucking white trash what are you thinking, you are disrespecting your colour" she spat out her words of hate at him and looked disgusted into his face.

"You are just a racist jealous vile and evil woman and I want you to leave and never come here again do you hear me?" he stood solid and looked like he meant what he said, he was no longer going to back down from her and wanted her to understand it.

"You fucking touch me I will report you for rape, you hit me and tried to rape me, I can be very convincing as you know, remember our roll play lover" she smirked at him and turned to walk away from him looking over her shoulder with a malevolent stare at him.

"Get out and stay out I am going to get a restraining order against you, you fucking psycho"

"Oh you think you bother me, you pathetic piece of shit" she laughed at him shaking her head as she did so turning back to face him.

"Just leave and leave me alone, it is over our life together is over" there was a hint of desperation in his voice and she honed in on it immediately.

"Oh are we getting upset" she mocked him laughing.

“Why have you come here, you have everything I cannot and do not need to give you anything, we are legally separated” his voice rose into an angry tone.

“I want money, you are keeping that little bitch of yours here, so you must be making it, I want money, you owe me”

“I owe you nothing, you are sick, you need bloody help woman”

She turned away from him again and said something he could not hear, she he put his hand on her shoulder to turn back to face him.

She quickly spun around and took something from the pocket of her dress. It was a small aerosol looking can and she sprayed it directly into his face. The pepper spray hit him full on for a few seconds and she laughed as he backed up his hands to his face and his eyes streaming. He staggered back and dropped to his knees he coughed out, and then without warning she turned and kicked him hard under the chin with the toe of her high heels boots. He reeled back blinded and disorientated.

“Not so fucking big and tough now, is you” she laughed slowly walked over to where he was struggling to see and stand. She kicked at him again and repeatedly stamped her high heels down at his head the steel tip of the heel leaving deep marks and cuts across his face.

He put his hands up to protect himself but she was relentless and stomped down and dug the heels in deep penetrating his skin and flesh, he screamed out as one of his eyes were dug deep back into the socket and he was blinded. She laughed and was enjoying her power and joy she was getting from doing this wicked vile thing. Her violence was strong and driven her heart was black and she was having a good time inflicting damage and pain on this man she once shared her life with. The same one who gave her everything and tried to make her happy but nothing he did or gave her was enough for her narcissist ways. Now she hated him resented him and wanted him dead. Not fearing any consequences she wanted him dead, kicking and stamping down onto his head and body she was building into frenzy when he suddenly lashed out in defence and knocked her back and over. This just infuriated her even more and she scrambled to her feet once again and came dashing forward. Evil in her eyes and the devil in her soul she tore bite and scratched at him with all her power and full force. He was blinded and the pepper spray incapacitated him he could not defend himself she scratched at his eyes and kicked and punched him like a mad woman screaming as she did. Eventually he was unconscious, knocked out cold then she pounded at his head stamping at his throat and face with her boots she didn't stop until he was lifeless and his head just a red pulp of flesh and brain matter. She had smashed his skull and his face, blood covering the carpet and his face torn to pieces. Eventually she stopped, out of breath and panting hard. Putting her hands on her knees she bent over getting her breath back. Then stretching up and back, she smiled and started to laugh. Moving over and stepping over the body she took deep breaths and felt good. No remorse no regret she acted as if nothing had happened, going through to the small kitchen she took some paper towels and washed the blood from her legs and shoes. Straightening her dress and hair and taking another deep breath and seemed calm. Walking from the kitchen she took no more notice of the dead body on the ground, it was no more concern to her. She quietly left and went back to her car not feeling anything at all she felt no worry no regret or any concern. Starting her car up then quietly drove away and left the scene. Never able to explain what had really happened or came over her she would just say she lost control and was provoked, she would lie and try to manipulate like she always has done. But the darkness was to blame, the deep evil in her soul. It controlled her and she had no chance of stopping it, she would never understand it and could never explain it she would lie her way around and she would be seen by psychiatrists but never will it be totally explained. Probably put down to some mental illness, maybe she would be able to spend some time in a hospital and be "cured" by therapy and drugs but the true cause would never be known, the true culprit was there and always would be there the darkness the evil in people just waiting to be controlled.

CHAPTER TEN

It was cold and it was raining, the day had been a very hard one for working outside up on a roof putting down slates. A young Richard was tired and shivering, his fingers were numb. They had felted and nailed the lattes down on the roof the day before and now carried every slate up the ladder, it was an old fashioned way of doing it but that is the way his dad worked. Packing away the tools he made sure he had everything. The rain had been relentless all day and now they were going home it stopped. There was a break in the cloud a faint bit of blue sky could be seen but it did nothing to lift moral or spirits, they were wet and cold and uncomfortable.

"Typical pisses down all day now we clear up it stops" His dad said as he came round and doubled checked the tool bag Richard had just filled.

"You have to weather the weather whatever the weather" Richard said sniffing up.

"Aye that's the spirit lad, come on let's get home"

They both walked away from the building and off the garden of the house that they were reroofing. It was being renovated and Richard's dad had got the job of reroofing it. They headed for the bus stop and the bus home. Richard carried the tool bag which was getting heavier all the time. He was worn out but didn't let his father see it. He never complained and always got the job done. He walked with the same stride as his dad and kept up with him, both were dirty and looked like the hard day's work they had just done. It was not a long walk to the bus stop but it was long enough when you were tired and carrying a heavy bag of tools. They waited for about fifteen minutes until the bus finally came, it took them into town then they caught another bus home to the house. Richard was glad of the sight of the front door; he put the tools down into coal house at the side and locked the door as his dad walked in the house leaving him to it, he double checked the door then followed.

As always his mother knew what bus they were coming home on and had a meal already cooking for them. Richard went up stairs and got changed then had a strip wash in the small sink in the bathroom. His dad did the same down stairs in the kitchen sink. They never had a shower in the house and made do with a strip wash. They both cleaned up got changed and then headed down for their well earned food. The meal was simple a stew but it was more than welcomed. Both of them were starving and it was devoured quickly with plenty of bread on the side. Not a lot was said, it never was at the dinner table. His dad finished first and stood up stretched out and went to sit in his chair by the open fire. His mother started to clear away the dishes while Richard finished his food and was still hungry but knew there was no more to be had. He was aching and was tired; he stretched out and finished the water in his glass.

"Give your mother hand lad" his dad said, Richard stood up and didn't question and went into the kitchen to help his mother with the dishes.

"Don't worry love, you can leave it I will do it, he will be asleep in a minute anyway" his mother told him, as she was putting some hot water into the sink.

"Go and rest mum you have made it I will clear it" Richard said ignoring what she had said.

"You are a good lad I have brought you up right, there may be many things wrong in this life but I got you right I know that" she said smiling at him as he filled the sink full of water.

"Whatever I am you made me mother, good breeding obviously" he said smiling at her.

"You are destined for great things I can see it, your life will become special my son. I know you will do great things maybe not always noticed but you will do the right thing at the right time. That is integrity and you will thrive and you go your own way"

"Whatever you say mum" he started to pull the dishes into the sink and stopped his mother from helping him; she smiled at him and let him do what he wanted to do.

"Life is about the person you become, you will come across bad people and good people, storms and sunshine, but remember a storm isn't always disruptive. It sometimes just clears the path to a better place"

"You are getting very philosophical mum" he said looking at her and could not help but smile while he did.

"Well Richard I have a very strong feeling, a very powerful vision about you, I see it more each day I see you maturing more each day. There is a very bad and large world out there son. You have to be ready to face it. Never judge someone by their words, they can say things easily. It's the actions you need to look at, see what they do not what they say"

Richard carried on with the washing up and looked at his mother who was stood by his side she was small in stature but he always felt the large powerful and strong woman she was. Taking a tea towel she started to rinse then dry off the pots he was washing.

"Well I will always keep in mind what you say mum, you are the strongest and wises woman I know that is for sure" he nodded in appreciation at his own words.

"Oh I don't know about that but someday some girl will come along and steal your heart no doubt, we have to go through pain to understand happiness. Just remember I will always be here for you son, no matter what happens no matter when it is I will always be here for you”

“Thanks mum, could have done with you today on that roof it was bloody freezing”

They both laughed and he felt good, he was tired and worn out but he felt good stood here talking to his mother it always made him feel happy and loved and wanted and safe. His mother smiled at him and shook her head she was proud and happy she had such a child.

After they had done the dishes and cleared up they both came into the front room. His father was asleep and snoring his chair. Richard sat down with a thud on the settee as his tired muscles and body made screamed out for rest. His mother came and quietly sat next to him.

“Thanks’ for letting me have this time off mum” he said to her.

“Well back to school next week lad, I didn’t want your father doing this job by himself, he is not getting any younger and needs more help really” she looked over with concern in her eyes at her husband asleep and looking tired slumped in his chair.

“I don’t mind helping him when I can, the money is nice too” he smiled at her and she smiled back at him then she looked again over at his Father.

“I know love I know, I just wish he didn’t have to work so hard. I wanted to get a part time job you know, but he wouldn’t let me, to proud and old fashioned I expect”

“I don’t blame him, I would not want you working either, it is the man’s job to provide for his family, you do enough and have done enough. We will look after you mum don’t worry all will be good and right in the world”

“Not the way this bloody world is going, I see it more and more on the news and in the papers, people are getting selfish violent and greedy. There seems to be no loyalty or self respect or dignity anymore. Everyone out for what they can have for themselves. Times are changing and I don’t like the way they are going” she sounded genuinely worried and Richard reached out to touch her arm reassuringly.

“Don’t worry mum I will protect you, no one will bother you while I am around”

“Oh I know that lad, and I will protect you too” she smiled at him but he could see a worry behind her eyes, she was aging and feeling the pain of her arthritis creeping in.

“We will fine, sod the world we will be fine” he said to her smiling.

“Life is hard love and you will learn many lessons along the way, the world is full of bad and evil things the devil is everywhere you just remember that and stay safe for me”

“I will mum if he comes near I will kick his arse back to where he came from”

“I am sure you will” she leaned over and hugged him and he could feel she held on to him a little tighter than normal. Something was bothering her deep inside and he could not put his finger on what it was. He was feeling tired and fatigue suddenly came over him. His eyes were heavy and he wanted to go to sleep. She eventually pulled away and looked into his tired eyes she knew he was worn out and she smiled at him widely.

“What?” he said looking at her smiling back at him?

“You look and are knackered”

“I am ok, would you like a cuppa, have we any biscuits?”

“No I am fine, why don’t you go for a nap you need it, you have had a gruelling day by the looks of it, and more tomorrow, you need your strength”

“What are you going to do?” he said standing up slowly and achingly with no intension of giving her any type of argument.

“I will watch a little TV your dad will be awake soon he only sleeps for about an hour, I will check in on you later to see if you want a drink or anything” she smiled at him and he smiled back then left the room. He walked up the stairs and felt the ache in his legs. He went to the toilet then collapsed onto his bed and was there asleep until early the next morning when he would be awoke by his dad telling him to hurry up they had work to do.

His mother sat quietly with her thoughts she held a small silver crucifix in her hand that was around her neck on a thin chain. She looked at her husband asleep in the chair and then she looked down and seemed to be in a world of her own. Her small and fragile shape sat quietly and still. Thoughts running through her head and her fingers gently and slowly rubbing the crucifix maybe unaware she was doing so. Her thoughts had taken her to another place and she was happy to be there at this moment. Eventually she lifted her head and looked up to the ceiling thinking of her son. She smiled and sighed out as she thought about him and then she looked at her husband asleep in the chair, these two men in her life was her whole life and she looked after them unselfishly and relentlessly. Not caring for her own happiness she was happy doing for them what she did. She gained happiness in knowing she was doing a good job in looking after her husband and bringing up a fine son. It was enough it was her life and it made her smile. She had been unloved when she had been put in the children's home. She always said if she had children of her own she would show them more love then she ever had and would make sure their life was happy and full of laughter. Sighing she watched her husband sleeping slouched in his chair and she gain glanced up to where her son had left the room.

CHAPTER ELEVEN

Travelling fast the darkness undetected moved across the land like a dangerous virus no one knew about. Contaminating anything it touched or controlling anything evil it desired. It was close, it knew it was close it could feel Stephanie and Richard, quickly it moved relentless across the land unseen un-heard and unhindered. Passing by the two girls sat on the wall it was there then gone. But it left the hate and the violence in them multiplied to a tremendous amount.

"I fucking hate her" The tall black skinny girl said to her friend with disgust.

"I know, I don't know who she thinks she fucking is, just because she got highest marks in class, so fucking what?" Her smaller and chubbier friend added.

"I think she is fucking the head that is why she gets top marks all the fucking time"

"Err gross, imagine that, no thank you" her friend said shaking her head.

"Well I hate the bitch; hate the sight of her" she huffed out and spat on the ground in front of her. They were both made up with far too much makeup on and had that annoying know it all attitude teenagers have. But this was more it was pure hate, a vengeful hate that had just multiplied tenfold. Dressed in ripped jeans and baggy top they had a jackets open and ripped at the pockets, it was hard to see what sort of style they were trying to pull off but whatever it was, it was not working for either of them.

"I think she needs a lesson in manners and that fucking smirk wiped off her ugly face if you ask me, I think she needs to be brought down a bit and knocked off that high horse of hers" The chubby girl said with a smirk and a sly look towards her friend.

"What have you in mind you wicked bitch, I love whatever it is already" they both laughed and leaned forward as they did. Looking up and down the street they giggled. The chubby girl took out a small lighter and flicked it to ignite the gas they watched the flame together then looked at each other and laughed out loud.

"Charlotte you are a genius" the tall girl said.

"Why thank you Gina, I do try" they both laughed again and jumped off the wall, they headed down the street then walked off by a opening that lead into the field and down towards the small wooded area.

"Do you think she will be still here?" Gina asked as they walked along.

"She spends hours down here bloody painting flowers and crap we have seen her before and I know she was here about an hour ago I saw her, so if she is we shall have some fun"

“You are now talking my language girl, I want to kick the shit out of the stuck up cunt, God I hate her and everything about the posh bitch I hate her”

“We shall take her down a peg or two and make sure that fucking smirk stays off her stupid ugly face” both girls laughed and quickened their pace. Heading down the small pathway they went into the trees. As they did they became quiet and slowly made their way towards the clearing where Charlotte had seen the girl earlier, they both stood silent when they caught sight of her. She had her back to them and was sat on a fallen log. A sketch pad in her hand and she was busy sketching some flowers by her feet.

A quiet pretty looking girl with long hair that was cut neatly in a fringe she was engrossed in her hobby and enjoying what she loved to do, sketch and draw. She was wearing a flowery dress that was out of fashion and old fashioned but she didn’t care she liked it and it was comfortable. This was her time and her little world; she became lost and was happy here. It was quiet and away from the hustle and bustle of life. It calmed her and made her at peace. She had no idea she was being watched and the two girls were quite close now. They hid down behind some fallen trees out of sight.

“What is she doing?” Charlotte asked quietly in a whisper.

“Drawing something the boring bitch, fuck I hate her” Gina spat out her words.

Both girls looked around the area and made sure no one was about then they looked at each other and nodded and smiled and both stood up and raced down towards their prey.

They came upon her fast and she had no idea there were there until they both crashed into her from behind. She was thrown forward and off her seated position. The drawing pad dropped down and the pencils scattered over the ground. Gina laughed out and kicked the girl in the side. Charlotte picked up the drawing and took out her lighter and set it on fire. This made both girls laugh and they watched as the drawing and the pad burnt away and was dropped onto the ground in flames.

"What the hell are you doing" The girl shouted as she staggered back up to her feet confused and feeling the pain in her ribs where she had been violently kicked.

"We are going to give Tracy Summers a fucking lesson, oh that's you isn't it?" Gina said looking as innocent as she could then she slapped Tracy across the face hard which reeled her back and she fell over again.

"Stop, what have I done stop this please" Tracey pleaded from the ground where she had been knocked back.

"Stop this please" Charlotte mocked in a sarcastic voice.

"Why are you doing this I have not done any of you any harm leave me alone"

“Shut the fuck up you stuck up bitch, oh I am top in art class, I am top in English I am top in every fucking thing, you fucking retard” Gina said mockingly looking for support from Charlotte which she got instantly with a laugh and a thumbs up sign.

Tracy said no more, if she was top in everything and this girl thought she was a retard then that told her all she needed to know about the logic and intelligence of this girl.

“Stand up you fucking slut” Charlotte shouted at her. Tracy stood up and looked around waiting for a chance to run.

“So you are fucking the head teacher are you, that is why you get top marks all the time isn’t it” Gina said coming close and putting her face in front of Tracy’s until their noses were touching. Tracy winced at the bad breath and body odour she could smell from this girl.

“No, I am not fucking anybody” Tracy looked at them both and just wanted to be away from them as soon as possible.

“Not surprised you fucking freak, look at you in old grannies dress” Charlotte said coming next to her and boxing her in between them.

“What do you want, let me go” Tracy insisted but was punched hard in the face by Gina and then Charlotte took one of her arms and pulled it up to the side, Gina did the same and they pulled out until Tracy was stood like she was being crucified. They pulled and stretched out until Tracy screamed with pain she was not strong enough to resist and they knew it. Shaking her head Tracy cried out again she didn't see Charlotte take out her lighter and come forward. She put the lit flame at the base of Tracy's hair and it caught fire. Both girls then pulled away and held Tracy at arm's length pulling out her arms to the side. Her hair caught fire wildly and it burned quickly. Smoking and smelling bad, Tracy screamed out and struggled frantically as she felt her hair ignite and her head burn.

Gina was laughing out loud she was almost crying with tears and Charlotte watched wide eyed for a moment at the ferocity of the flames then she started to laugh as well. Shaking in panic and pain Tracy struggled and then felt the kick to her stomach which knocked the wind out of her she was let go and collapsed to the ground in pain. She rolled about patting her head frantically and crying hysterically with panic.

Her two tormentors just stood and watched her, laughing they were genuinely amused and then came forward and started to kick at their victim as she rolled around on the ground. Her head smouldering and tears rolling down her face, Tracy knew she had to do something these cruel girls were not going to stop. Why they had attacked her she didn't know but she could not just let then torture and kick her like this. She rolled away and picked up one of her pencils she had been drawing with that she had dropped when they attacked her.

Dodging away from their kicks she moved quickly and stabbed the sharp pencil hard and deep into Gina's leg. Gina screamed out and staggered back startling Charlotte for a moment, and then she was served with the same treatment.

Tracy had picked up a second pencil and as she stood up she stabbed it as hard as she could into Charlottes shoulder just under the collar bone. It went in very deep and Charlotte grabbed out at Tracy pulling her down as she did. Both girls rolled about fighting on the ground. Gina limped forward cursing and started to punch down at Tracy who was now on top of Charlotte fighting for her life. She was punching and scratching in a frenzy of survival. Gina hit her and then was surprised that Tracy turned and hit her back, she had found strength in fear and knew she had to fight her way out of this. Knocking Gina back Tracy punched again at Charlottes blooded face. She then staggered to her feet, adrenaline keeping her going. Turning she saw Gina pull the pencil from her leg and holding it like a knife ready to stab down at her with it.

"Why, why are you doing this?" Tracy shouted not understanding why it was all happening.

"You are fucking dead, fucking dead" Gina shouted out and came forward in a crazed state of rage. Charlotte reached up and pulled at Tracy's dress knocking her off balance a little and distracting her just enough to give Gina time to stab the pencil into Tracy's eye, it went in very deep through the eye ball through soft flesh and into the brain. Tracy dropped to her knees, she felt weak she felt dizzy and disorientated.

Gina fell over with the momentum she had given herself as she lunged forward. Landing next to a blooded Charlotte they both looked on as Tracy swayed on her knees, bloody coming from her eye socket and a low moan from her throat. The seriousness of it all suddenly hit home and both girls watched as Tracy seemed to be getting slower and slower until she finally just keeled over and was still, the pencil still protruding from her eye socket.

"You have fucking killed her you have killed her" Charlotte screamed at Gina, who was still looking at Tracy's still body. Eventually Gina smiled then a little nervous laugh then she turned to Charlotte and smiled.

"We have done it and no one will ever know we were not seen and we need to get away, you tell no one about any of this do you fucking hear me" Gina grabbed Charlotte by the shoulders and glared her in the eye. Charlotte nodded scared and nervously and started to breath erratically.

"Ok, yeah lets run" Charlotte said and started to stand up.

“Evidence, fire it gets rid of all evidence we need to burn the body, my finger prints are on that pencil”

“Fuck that, I am gone” Charlotte insisted pulling away from Gina’s grip and standing up.

“Come here you little cunt” Gina violently grabbed Charlotte and shook her by the shoulders.

“Leave me alone” Charlotte shouted at her as panic started to rise within her guts.

“You are in this just as much as me, don’t you forget that, we are in this together, you can go to prison and you will die there, we need to get this sorted out and get away” Gina shouted at her to make her hear what she was saying.

“Quickly lets be quick I don’t want to be here fuck sake, fuck” Charlotte said wiping the blood from her face where she had been hit in the nose.

Gina gingerly walked over to Tracy’s body and looked down at the still state it was in she could not tell if she was breathing or not. She looked over at Charlotte who was shaking and looking around she wanted to be gone. Reaching down and breathing heavy Gina reached for the pencil and tried to pull it out but it was stuck. She took a deep breath and let it back out erratically. Her hands were shaking and she tried again the blood was all over Tracy’s face and her head was bleeding and badly burnt she looked lifeless but suddenly she moaned and her hand came up quickly grabbing hold of Gina's arm. Charlotte screamed and shook riveted for a moment to the spot, Gina screamed and tried to pull her harm away.

"Help me" Gina shouted to Charlotte but was horrified when she saw her friend turn and run off away in a panic. Looking back down she saw Tracy looking at her through a wide open eye and she froze with fright. Tracy fumbled for something on the ground and found the large thick pencil she brought it up and around stabbing repeatedly into Gina's neck, blood pumped out at an alarming rate and Gina fell back clutching her hands to the red blooded gash in her neck. She staggered and felt weak so much blood was pumping out of the artery that had been punctured and damaged. She could do nothing to stop it she shook as the sight of the ground turning red her clothes and the torrent of her own blood flowing down her arm. She dropped to her knees felt dizzy felt weak and then dropped face first into the dirt.

Both girls were still, the girls were dead, Charlotte would be left to explain but how she would explain it would never really be enough. The darkness had touched them and no matter what she says no matter how she tried to explain it no one would really understand. Her life was ruined and the life of her friend was over, a poor innocent girl was dead and the effect it would have on her family would never be overcome and never be understood. Mindless and senseless it left a scar that would never heal and a life taken far too early. The darkness, that was to blame, but no one will ever know no one could know. Hell had touched them this day and it would be forever in their mind.

CHAPTER TWELVE

Richard stopped by the small stone church he had not been back here for many years. It stood alone in its own small enclosed grounds. None descript but strangely engaging as you looked at it. There was something about the little building that was in front of you that you could not quite put your finger on, something that seemed to draw your attention and hypnotic. The old grey slate roof was in good condition but well weathered much like the whole building but it was still strong and solid. The small slatted windows on each side had stain glassed still in them; it was hard to tell if the place was still used. The grass around it seemed short and cut and the area looked litter free and clean, there was nothing else in its small walled grounds, just a small enclosure and pathway to the front entrance. Fields on either said and a cluster of trees to the back, it was not too far from the town but far enough. Richard seemed and was lost with his own thoughts while he was looking at it.

"Is this the church, is this where she used to come?" Stephanie asked looking at it already knowing the answer.

"Yes, it was a twenty minute walk from our house to get here; she used to do it often this place meant something to her she was always at peace here. I remember when she was very old and weak.

She still insisted on making the journey here, I drove her then of course" he said not taking his eyes from the old oak wooden door at the front.

"It meant so much to her, this is a special place Richard, can you feel that, can you sense the power emanating from that small place?" Stephanie smiled she knew its greatness and she could feel the force that was here.

"I feel a lot of things, and one of them is hunger, let's go eat somewhere"

"Hold on we must go in, we must see what..."

"We will go in later I am hungry and we need food" he said not looking at her and pulled off slowly heading down the quiet road. Stephanie stared at him and tried to understand his reaction but she could not. He was a very deep and secretive man she always knew this, but there was something now that she had not seen or felt before coming from him. He was delving back into his past, reaching far behind him and remembering this time. It was a place no one had ever been allowed before. She could only imagine what was going through his mind right now. It was a time after them but before anyone who Richard knows now ever existed in his life; it was his past his time and his memory she decided to let him have his own and alone time with it. Looking out of the window she watched the stone wall race past her as they drove along, noticing the large fields beyond and then up to the horizon, lifting her gaze up to the dull sky she wondered if his Mother was looking down and watching them.

She was awaked from her daydream when Richard suddenly started to talk.

"The trouble these days is people are to bloody sensitive and soft and weak. I have always said it I have seen it, the world will self destruct eventually, too much greed and selfishness. These are winning the battle and the generation that is coming up now will do nothing to stop it, because they are lazy and want everything for free. Don't want to work for it just give me it I want it and if they don't get it they throw a tantrum until they do" He shook his head and clicked his tongue.

"Like I said before, it is the way of the world we will not change it, there is much we know that most people will never understand or realise, the darkness will always be there to feed on the feeble and take advantage of their inner demons and weaknesses. You need to understand Richard all this will still be here when we are gone. You have to take the chance of happiness if it presents its self to you. Please promise me if you see the light, if you see the chance for happiness you will take it. You owe this world nothing but this world owes you much" she turned to look at him and could see he was thinking about what she was saying.

"What do you mean if it presents its self to me?" he asked without looking at her.

"I don't know but we are doing something we have never done before, you are delving back further then you ever have, in your adult life, something is happening and whatever it is you must be ready for it"

"I was born ready" he said half joking.

"I am serious this is bigger than anything before, it must be a sign it must mean something like never before surly you realise that now?"

He glanced over at her and held the stare for a few seconds then looked back forward but said nothing. They drove along in silence until he stopped the vehicle and looked up at a semi detached house. It was up from the road and had stone steps going from the pavement to the front. He looked and scanned the whole area and along the row of houses across the road, the pathway to the large field to the back. Stephanie could see the memories flashing through his eyes and into his brain she knew this was the place he grew up.

"That small window there, on the right side, that was my room" he finally said looking up at the house.

"It feels strange but I feel like I have been here before, this is where you came to live?"

"After my dad died she moved to a smaller place about a mile away, you have not been here before, no one has ever been here before" he said solemnly

"So this is your home ground, your place of adventure when you were a child after us eh?"

"We used to make carts from old pram wheels, and a board, the front wheels on a cross bar with string tied to each end, that was to steer, bogies we used to call them. Came racing down that field to the back, down this little gap between them two houses there, and into the road, straight across and down that dirt track that lead to the farm below. You stopped when you hit something, most of the time a bloody stone wall at the bottom, it is a sharp bend and we never made it. Just crashed and pulled it back up and started again."

"What if there was a car coming?" Stephanie said seeing what he was pointing at, the field behind the house, the gap between two houses and then into the road across it and down the dirt track. She tried to imagine kids racing down here and having no regard for their safety as they raced each other in their home made carts of wood and pram wheels.

"I used to sit on the window sill looking out of that small window early in the morning. Silence except for the sounds of nature. The sound of it was peace and harmony to me then when I started to hear the traffic and see people I closed the window and went back to bed"

She looked at him and let him drift away for a moment with his memories, he looked down the road and then back up it. Looking back at Max Richard sighed and got out of the vehicle he stretched and opened the door to let Max out. Stephanie knew she could not stop him he was to head strong. So just went with it although she knew the urgency they were facing she decided to let him do what he does, and that was things his own way.

"Let's have a walk then we eat then we make plans" he said as she came next to him, he locked up his vehicle and headed off across the road. They all walked up the grassed gap between the houses and in to the large field behind. It banked up and he seemed to know where he was going. Max ran off ahead and checked everything as he always does smelling and scenting as he went along. There had been a pathway here at some point but it was over grown now, it looked like not many people came along here anymore. He headed up and walked along where the pathway would have been in his day. Stopping he turned and looked down to the rear of the row of houses and stared at his old house. Stephanie stood next to him and looked out across the field down to the houses and up beyond to another housing estate a few miles in the distance.

“This is your old stomping ground then is it?” she asked feeling calm and strangely unrushed all of a sudden. This was a very rare moment and she was going to digest it.

“Yeah this was the back field, it’s all over grown now, not like it was, kids probably never come here, they never bloody play outside any more do they, stick indoors playing stupid games or on the computers” he sighed

“The world changes and people change, it can never just stay the same. What was down there?” she pointed off into the distance where there had obviously been a building but now was gone, it was fenced off and she could still see the outlines in the clearing.

“A school, Guardhouse it was called, I used to go there and walk up and across here at dinner time, I came home for dinners my mum could not afford school dinners”

“You walked home every dinner time?”

“Yes, we didn’t have much and a school dinner was a luxury we could not afford”

“Take a pack lunch?” Stephanie was a little surprised at his statement.

“There used to be a bloody big dead tree here He turned and pointed to a spot behind them. I used to climb it when I was a kid and eventually it blew down one night when we had very strong winds. Me and my dad got the bow saws and came up to saw it up for the fire, it did us for quite a while that did" he smiled and looked back down at the house again.

Max was rolling on his back and twisting about on the grass nearby he didn't seem to have a care in the world, just like his master. Stephanie looked round once again and knew this place was so powerful because it held so much of Richard Cushing's past and it was here, where he was forged and made into the man he is today.

"So you burnt wood on your fire?"

"We only had one open fire in the whole house that was the means of all the heating and the back boiler was what gave us the hot water. It was one of my jobs to make sure we had wood for it, I used to go out and get it from where ever I could and sawing odd branches from trees sometimes, carrying them home and splitting the logs. We managed and if not we put extra clothes on to keep warm.

"Bloody hell Richard you make it sound like the nineteen forties you grew up in, was you all behind the times?" Stephanie said with a slight smile but regretted saying it quickly.

"My dad was old fashioned and a working class man, he made sure we had food and shelter and that was his main priority in life. It was all he knew how to do, kids these days would fucking die if they had to live like we did. But it gave you respect it gave you thankfulness and it made you appreciate things, I would not change it if I had to go back"

"I am sorry I didn't mean to sound impertinent" she bit her lip and cursed herself but didn't show it she just looked out across the field and down to his old house.

"Not many people understand but working class northern folk did, like you said the world is changing and things are being forgotten, disrespect and egotism are the norm. I don't like this world anymore Stephanie and this world doesn't like me"

"You take whatever chance presents itself Richard" she said putting her hand on his shoulder and looking at him as he turned to face her.

"I used to come up here in summer or spring whatever and lay down on my back looking up to the clear blue sky, there used to be a bird I am not sure what it was called I think it was a sky lark but I could be wrong. Anyway it used to go really high and just seemed to hang there, chirping or whistling away it was a great thing to see and feel. There seemed to be no one else on the planet and this bird was chirping and singing away for you to enjoy. How things change when you get older and how your memories hold you to the past"

“Well we all have them, and they are what connects you to your past, just enjoy the happy ones that make you smile and remember the good times”

“The trouble is the bad ones always creep in and bugger it up” he sighed and looked round one last time and then turned to Stephanie and smiled a little smile.

“Are you alright?” she asked him a little curious what might be going on in his head.

“It’s time we made a move and made plans to deal with what is coming Stephanie, what are you not telling me; there is something that doesn’t quite jell here?”

“I have told you everything, all what you are feeling you are feeling for a reason, you have to go back to be able to go forward and win this thing. I have one purpose and that is to save you, please believe me all your past must come forward and defend you now. What is coming will not stop, it already knows I am doomed but it is you that it wants. You are the prize it is after and nothing will stop it, it will take you. Like I told you before everything it touches it will control and it will control everything to destroy you” she was calm but serious a worried look was deep in her eyes and he stared at her for a long moment.

"You are doomed, you can't be saved?" He asked her as she bowed her head and shook it for a moment, then looked up at him with tears in her eyes.

"I don't think anything or anyone can help me now I can't escape it, but this is about you, not me. Please heed to what your heart is telling you to all the things you are remembering here Richard. This place made you who you are and the answer is here. It is the only place that really knows you. The only place that can help you, the only power that is strong enough is here, and it know s it will do anything to stop you"

"If we have the power to defeat it here why can that not help you, why can you not be saved also lass?" He was staring her in the eyes and she felt it straight to her soul, his deep blue eyes were intense and she shuddered but didn't know why.

"This is about you not me, you are the one to be saved not me, you have a choice and a chance and you must take it, you must let the only person strong enough pure enough and powerful enough help you Richard" her voice was almost beseeching with him.

"I am not exposing her to this fight to this evil it is my fight and we can do this together"

She shook her head and pushed him back with both hands in anger.

"For God's sake listen to me, she is the only one, the only one do you hear, it is no good shutting out your past and locking it behind that door and throwing away the key. You must invite her back into your life she will come and is the only thing strong enough to help you; you really don't have a choice. Can you not see can you not really see what is happening, what about the old man by her grave side, the crucifix?" she pleaded with him and sighed out in frustration. He reached into his pocket and took out the small silver cross. He looked at it and then looked at Stephanie who was staring at him expectantly.

"You must see it Richard that is why you are here, that is why all your childhood memories have come back to you, and you are here for a reason. That reason is to reconnect so she can help you, like she always did and it is your only chance. Nothing else, not even you, can stop this thing it is concentrated evil and it commands all evil"

He put the crucifix back in his pocket and held Stephanie to him she welcomed the show of affection and dropped her head into broad chest. She could hear his strong heat beat and closed her eyes. He looked down towards his old house. He looked across to where the school used to be. Then he heard it, it was a sound he had not heard since he was a child, yes definitely that was it he thought. A sky lark rising up into the sky, but it was out of season?

He watched and he listened to the chirping song and it made him smile. He remembered lying in this very field listening to this bird and he smiled wider. What it meant he didn't know but he was fixed on the small dot in the sky above him and he felt the memory of that sound. Taking a deep breath Stephanie felt his chest rise and fall she didn't want to let go and became worried once again. What if she could not convince him of the impending danger, what if he just tried to fight it head on like he always did?" she held him a little tighter until he gently moved back and pushed her from him. He looked at her and smiled his smile.

"Let's eat lass and then we can sort out what the hell we are going to do"

They walked away and out of the field back to the vehicle Bode was let in first. He drove away saying nothing but Stephanie could sense something different. She could see he was thinking more along the lines of what she was saying and it pleased her. She didn't know how she could sense it but she knew she could. Hoping he finally understood she sat back in her seat and wiped her eyes.

CHAPTER THIRTEEN

Dog fights are illegal and Logan had no respect for the law anyway so didn't care. He was a scrawny man with tattoos all over his pencil thin arms. Driving his old for transit van down the duel carriageway he was chewing on something and it made him look even uglier than he already was. Short greasy hair and unshaven he had body odour and black teeth. He had lived on welfare all his life and used the system all he could. Sat next to him was his girlfriend of four years Gail. She was overweight and smelt worse than he did, dressed in a top that was too small for her and jeans that were too big she had a large cat on her knee and was stroking it gently as she looked out of the window straight ahead.

"He better fucking turn up this time the wanker, my dogs are itching for a good fight" Logan said not taking his eyes from the road ahead.

"Yeah" was all Gail said as she glanced over her shoulder and saw two pit bull terriers sat up in the back of the van they had a chain around their neck which acted like a collar. Muscular and vicious looking being bread for fighting, scares on their body and face told tales of past battles and fights won and lost.

"I lost out on good money last time, he knows my dogs will kill anything he brings that is why he is shy of coming back for more, fuck, yeah my babies ripped his fuckers to bits last time" he smiled and shouted "fuck" as he drove nodding his head in glee.

"I hope we make some money Logan we need some money" Gail said looking back out of the window and stroking her cat that seemed unconcerned two savage beasts were right behind it, it stayed calm and sat content in her lap.

"Oh shut the fuck up we will make money, fuck me is that all you are concerned about?" he spat out his words in a disgusted and violent manner

"No of course not, just be nice that is all?" she defended weakly.

"Shut the fuck up and stroke your pussy" he said shaking his head and spitting something out on the floor of the van as he drove along he then wiped his mouth with the back of his hand.

He turned off the duel carriage way and went down towards a roundabout. Then looking at the signs he tried to figure out which way to go. Squinting at the signs he eventually turned left and headed off about a mile down the road until he turned off down a quieter road and eventually leading onto a more rural dirt track.

"Is it the farm, again, are we going to that smelly farm place again" Gail asked screwing her face up at the thought of it.

"Yes and don't give me any shit about it, and keep that fucking cat under control"

"I have to bring her; she gets lonely being left by herself"

"Fuck me, it's a fucking cat it doesn't give a fuck about you, you stupid cow, it is a vicious thing and doesn't like anybody"

"Shut up stop being mean to me all the time" she pulled her cat closer towards her and shot him a dirty glance as she did.

He sighed out and slowed down as the track got worse and he had to avoid holes and rocks along the way. The dogs in the back were getting thrown about a bit as the van rocked along the uneven ground and Logan's driving left a lot to be desired.

"Fucking track, the road is up here again in a minute" he said as he struggled the van along the uneven and unused track.

"It's making me feel sick" Gail said swallowing and putting her hand out to steady herself as the van lunged to one side then back again.

"Stop your winging" Logan shouted as he fought to keep the van on the track then eventually he headed out and on to tarmac again and was driving away.

They drove faster and headed off towards the old farm house that was now illegally used for the dog fights. Logan had trained his two dogs to be merciless and vicious he had been fighting them for over a year now and enjoyed the sick thrill of seeing them rip another poor dog to bits and kill it more than not. He made money out of it and spent the money of drugs and booze as soon as he got it. He didn't care about anyone except himself and Gail was now getting on his nerves he had already made plans to kick her out soon. He drove fast and passed through a slight small pocket of darkness that seemed to be travelling the other way. He paid it no notice it was not important he had a place to be and was eager to see his dogs in action. The cat that Gail had on her knee was suddenly stiff, its supple body and welcoming demur suddenly changed and it started to shake. Gail felt it and looked down curious at what was happening she had never seen or felt her cat do this before.

"Something is wrong with Twinkle?" she said looking across to Logan.

"What, what the hell you on about?" he snapped back not looking at her and speeding up.

"She has gone all stiff, she is shaking, something is wrong with her?" Gail said worried and tried to stroke her cat which suddenly without warning bared its teeth and scratched her viciously across the hand and snarled at her arching its back and the fur stood up, its claws came out and dig deep into her legs. She screamed out more in fear then in pain.

"What the fucking hell" Logan shouted as he looked over and saw the cat dive for Gail's face, and then bite and scratch at it. She screamed and tired to pull the cat off her but it was in frenzy and was screeching and scratching and digging its teeth into her without mercy and with intensity. Gail screamed and tried to fight the cat off but it was relentless.

The two dogs barked and started to move about in the back and Logan didn't know what to do he reached over and tried to pull the cat off her but it turned on him as he did and pounced onto his lap digging its claws in deep then jumping up at his face. He held his hands up to protect himself and lost control of the van. It veered off the road and he fought to try recover it but he had lost the battle the van slammed down the incline and off into the small field that banked to the left the van tilted and ran over uneven ground too fast tilting up and turning over onto its side with a thud and violent jerk as it came to a quick stop.

Gail was screaming and holding her face she was blinded and could not see anything her eye balls had been scratched and damaged beyond repair. The two back doors were buckled and flew open as the van came to a sudden haul on its side in the small field. The two pit bulls were thrown out somewhere and Logan was on his side still fighting this insane cat off which was still attacking without mercy. He managed to grab it and bash it against the steering wheel he smashed it hard and then threw it into the back. He held his face and his head which was cut, bleeding badly, moaning loudly he grunted out his pain.

“Logan I can’t see, Logan” Gail said out in panic. But her words were ignored he didn’t care. He scrambled over her and out of the back of the van and shook his head trying to see clear again. He rolled out onto the grass and looked around for the demented cat but it seemed to have run off. Taking deep breaths he sat on the ground for a moment and tried to compose himself. Blood was on his hands and over his face he could feel it dripping off his chin. He rolled over moaning and staggered to his feet. He looked back and saw his precious van on its side steaming water pouring from the front and the whole vehicle buckled.

He cursed and kicked out at the grass with anger and annoyance. He then noticed the two sets of eyes looking at him. His two dogs were sat close by and staring at him motionless and silent they watched him as he swayed unsteady in front of them. Wiping the blood from his face he tried to focus his eyes on the two animals.

“Logan help me, where are you” Gail was crying out but he ignored her and heard her scrambling about in the van blindly.

“Fuck off, both of you just go, go on fuck off” Logan said as he uneasily looked at his fighting dogs looking at him in a way that made him nervous. He lifted his head and searched the area, there was no one or nothing around them he still had at least a mile to reach the farm yet. Swallowing he rubbed his brow with the back of his hand and stepped back taking deep breaths. He was breathing heavy and shaking uncontrollably. He stepped back again and started to edge away from the dogs that were motionless and staring at him. Edging away he moved back and then turned and started run as fast as he could across the field. Taking deep breaths he sprinted with all his energy away from the scene and he hoped to safety.

The two fit and active dogs stood and watched him then without warning they both silently gave chase. They easily caught up with him and he was wheezing as they did he turned and saw them both pounce through the air and savagely bring him down. He had no chance and was ripped and tore to pieces. Their powerful jaws tore chucks of flesh from his body their teeth dug deep and ripped him open. He screamed and tried in vain to fight them off but he had no strength at the best of times and these two fighting beasts were showing no mercy just like he had trained them and beat into them. Keep going until the other one is dead he used to shout at them. It was over in less than a minute he was dead, ripped open and tore apart his throat gushing out blood. His lifeless body was left there as the two dogs looked back over to the van. Gail was managing to crawl out sobbing and scared and shaking. Blood still dripping from their mouths the two dogs calmly walked back towards the van and Gail. They would finish her the same way but she had no idea it was coming like Logan did, she was blinded to it and would know nothing until they were upon her which would be in less than thirty seconds. The cat was only twenty yards away it was sat silently watching as the dogs did what they did, unaffected the cat licked at its paws and fur then turned and walked away, the darkness had touched these animals but they didn't understand it and just took it as it was. It meant nothing to them and after today they would not give it anymore thought. The accident would not be fully explained but Logan would be put to blame with the drugs and alcohol in his blood stream, the dogs might be hunted down but that would be the end of it, no more explanation would be needed no one would really care.

The darkness was getting close to its target and moving steady silent un-noticed and savagely dangerous. The malevolent power drifting across the country side un-detected the ultimate power of evil hiding in plain sight for all to see but no one would know what it was. It touched things and it destroyed them and corrupted them never stopping and homing in on what it had come for. An unseen and unstoppable force of darkness that had one aim and it was a simple but devastating aim. To damage and bring devastation in its wake to hunt and destroy one man and corrupt whoever it touched on the way, it was simply hell on earth.

CHAPTER FOURTEEN

The pub was quiet and Stephanie was hungry she had ordered a big meal for them both and waited until Richard sorted Max out; they had said he was not allowed to come in so he had taken some water and food outside to him. The pub held a history for Richard and as he waited for Max to finish around the cobbled area by the back entrance it flashed back to him. It was an older place and his mother and father came here regularly. Comprising of two open rooms it still had the old feel of the old pubs from the past when they were popular meeting places; a real fire place was set but not lit most of the time only on very cold days was a roaring fire in the grate. The bar ran down one end of one room and the wooden floor was well worn and had a long indentation in it where people had stood over the years drinking or waiting to be served. It was normally a quiet respectable little pub. But on this occasion there were three brothers here and they were loud and arrogant.

"Noisy buggers have no respect"

"Don't worry about them Geoff" Richard's mother told her husband.

"I am telling ya mother they are pissing me off there is no need for it"

“You know who that is don’t you, its bloody Bentley, he used to go to school with our Richard that one, the whole bloody family are trouble makers”

“You mean he is the same age as our Richard twenty, he looks a lot older then bloody twenty?”

“Just ignore them they will leave soon enough”

Bentley and his two brothers were shouting at the top their voice at the bar sharing a joke no one else in the pub found funny. The bar staff were not wanting to be bothered with them because they already had a reputation around town as being trouble causers and best left alone. The rest of the pub was quiet and just wished they would leave, but Geoff was staring at them and wanted to go and sort them out, it was in his make up the way he had been brought up. He sighed out and finished his pint of beer in one gulp then stood up and took his glass towards the bar.

“Geoff, leave it for a moment please”

“Listen mother them buggers don’t scare me none” he smiled at his wife and walked to the bar only about six feet away from the rowdy threesome. The reluctant bar man came over and asked quietly what Geoff would like.

“Why are tha whispering ya berk?” Geoff asked and then told him he wanted a pint and a milk stout. The bar man said nothing and went to get his drinks. Bentley looked over and shouted at the bar man.

"Hey Wazak, three more and be quick about it"

"Yes won't be a moment just serving this gentlemen" the bar man said nervously suddenly noticing he was alone behind the bar as his colleague had gone mysteriously somewhere else. Bentley turned and looked at Geoff staring back at him.

"I don't see anyone, not unless you mean this old fossil he won't mind waiting"

Glaring threateningly towards Geoff, Bentley had a smirk on his face that Geoff wanted to knock right off. He felt his whole body tense up with inner rage.

"He is serving me, then you can have your lot" Geoff said knowing he had his wife here and there was three of them, but he was raging inside and struggling to keep a lid on it.

"What the fuck did you just say to me you old cunt?" Bentley turned to confront Geoff, who was a lot smaller and obviously older then he was. His two brothers came by his side and they all glared at Geoff who stood his ground and was not fazed.

"He is serving me then you can have your lot, are you fucking deaf?" Geoff said but knew it was a mistake; he just could not help himself.

Without warning Bentley punched Geoff in the eye hard, knocking him back but not down, blood splattered over his face from the cut and Geoff instinctively lashed back but was to slow and missed his target. Losing his balance he fell and as he did a vicious kick to the head from Bentley stung him into a daze.

"Stop, stop this" Richard's mother came running over and bent down to help her husband who was dazed on the floor blood running down his face.

"While you are down there love" Bentley said rubbing his crotch and putting it near to her face as he did, they all laughed out and he turned back around but before he did he pushed her over and she fell next to husband. She was shaking and scared but still trying to help him up. Geoff was fuming and shook his head he stood back up and picked up a heavy glass ash tray, the type they used to have in them days thick glass and a heavy weapon. But his wife stopped him and pulled him back she knew the large heavy glass ash tray would have done some serious damage and Geoff would not have hesitated to use it.

"Just leave, both of you go, leave" the bar man came over and told them, while he then turned to serve the Bentley brothers.

Geoff was reluctantly pulled away cursing and out of the pub by his wife. He was fuming, frustrated and angry and bleeding.

“What the fuck, why the fuck, bloody hell mother why?” he was shouting and trying to get too many words out at once.

“Let’s just go home, leave it Geoff, I have to fix that eye you are cut and bleeding love”

“Fucking wankers” Geoff was going to go back but his wife forcefully pulled him away and pushed him up the road. He went with her and was more upset that he had not done more. But he knew his wife was right, there was three of them and much younger. His pride was hurt but betters that, then his wife hurt he thought. She pulled out a hanky and wiped it on his bleeding eye; he took it from her and wiped the blood from his face. They went home in a taxi and she was glad to get in doors but soon it was to turn to dread again.

Richard was sat watching a documentary on the TV about a serial killer when he saw his parents walk in, he stood up instantly when he saw the swelling and cut eye of his father and the panic look on his mothers face.

“What happened?” he asked coming to help his father sit down in the chair. His mother went to get some water and a towel to clean him up.

“Fucking wankers” his dad said cursing under his breath again.

“Who what, tell me who did this, what is going on dad?” Richard insisted feeling his blood boil at seeing his father bleeding and hurt.

“Just leave it our Richard, it’s nothing it’s over now” his mother said as she came back in with a small first aid kit and a wet towel to wipe the blood away.

“Fucking wankers hit me and pushed ya mother t’ ground”

“Who did it?” Richard insisted and started to lose his temper and his voice raising.

“Love, it is over please no more trouble is needed” his mother said tending to her husband’s cut eye and she could see the bruising and swelling coming up.

“That wanker Bentley, and his brothers, if there had just been him I would of kicked the fucker into next week” Geoff said, much to his wife’s disapproval.

“Bentley did this where is he?” He said straightening up and taking a deep breath.

“The Commercial” his dad said and Richard was quickly out the door.

“Did you have to tell him that Geoff, did you have too?”

“Fucking wankers” Geoff said again anger on his face.

Richard was in his Ford Sierra and racing down towards the commercial pub within minutes; he knew Bentley from school and knew what he and his brothers looked like. There had been times when they had been threatening but Richard had always brushed it off. But now they had stepped over the line and they were going to find out what it meant to feel retribution. He brought the car to a skidding halt outside the back entrance of the pub and raced in through the small door and past the toilets and then into the main bar area. He searched round but could not see them he walked to the bar and insisted on the attention of the bar man.

"Bentley, where the fuck is he?" Richard asked aggressively.

"I don't know to be honest, he was in here then he left" The bar man said and Richard didn't like his nonchalance attitude so he grabbed him by the collar and pulled him over the bar towards his face quickly and violently.

"I will ask you one more bloody time"

"He left went across to the Rodney I think not sure, it was that way" the bar man said nervously and smiled a silly anxious smile.

He left and ran over the road towards the Rodney pub, he went in and searched round the place, he could not see them anywhere. Cursing he dashed into the men's toilets and checked in there but still nothing. Heading out the back door he quickly walked down through the grave yard he knew the Burlington arms pub was at the bottom. He was going to search every pub until he found them and didn't mind if it took him all day and night. Turning onto the road he walked the short distance and through the small car park at the front up the steps and into the top area of the small pub. He heard the laugh and the shouting and knew he had found his target. They had just got their drinks and were heading away from the bar on the left side. Richard jumped down the three steps and charged forward towards Bentley. He front kicked him hard and sent him reeling back over a small wooden table. The other customers scattered and a woman screamed. Bentley's brothers both came for him one from each side. Ducking Richard lashed out and caught one square on the jaw snapping it off its hinges, spinning the man to the ground awkwardly in pain and dazed then he passed out cold.

"Get out, stop it I am calling the police" a voice came from somewhere behind the bar but Richard ignored it and was focused on the men in front of him. Bentley cursed and got to his feet he saw his brother trying to smash his glass of beer into Richards head but he missed and Richard took him by the shoulders and head butted the man hard on the nose splitting it and jolting the man's head painfully back. Then he stepped back and kicked him square between the legs squashing his testicles with his boot as he did. The man screamed and dropped to the ground and Richard wasted no time he repeatedly hit and punched the man pounding him until he was unconscious. Dropping in a heap on the ground, bleeding from his nose mouth and cut face the man was out cold for some time.

Bentley came forward and kicked at Richard and then tried to dash away. Richard picked up a small wooden stool and threw it at Bentley's legs bringing him down and crashing into the small steps. He turned quickly and kicked out again at Richard who was moving in on him with a frightening look of hate on his face that scared Bentley to the core.

"Fuck off, just fuck off" Bentley shouted but it was falling on deaf ears. There was nothing he could say that would stop him now. The fight was vicious and both men hit out and kicked they got thrown about over tables and onto the floor. Everyone in the room had got out and the bar man was shouting at them but neither of them heard a word he was saying. Richard fought like a mad man the rage in him not letting him give in. He powered Bentley back and jabbed him hard in the face, blood and teeth spat out of Bentley's mouth as he staggered back. Richard dashed forward and kicked out catching Bentley on the knee. Painfully he wobbled and dropped for a moment, he still lashed out at Richard but it was no good he was on him and pounding him with punch after punch. Rolling away in a futile attempt to stand up Bentley cried out as several kicks broke his ribs. Richard grabbed his hair and pulled Bentley up and pulverized his fist into his already battered and bloody face.

“Stop the police are coming get away go” the desperate barman was shouting.

Richard hit hard and did a lot of damage to Bentley. He finally lifted the semi conscious body and breathing heavily shouted at Bentley’s face.

“If you ever touch my dad again if you ever touch my mother again I will come and fucking kill you do you fucking understand me?” he shouted it and waited for some sort of response from his battered and damaged adversary. He then lifted the head and rammed it down into the ground with great force and power knocking Bentley unconscious. Standing up he looked around at the other two who were both out of the fight. Then across to the bar man who was stood looking at Richard with his mouth open, and telephone receiver in his hand.

“I will call the police” he said nervously.

“Call the fucking morgue for all I care” he said and he left the pub. Bentley was never the same again, he suffered multiple fractures broken ribs lost teeth. A broken cheek bone and severe concussion. His jaw had been broken in three places and the traumatic effect made him a nervous wreck. Richard was never reported and he never heard anything more about it. But the reputation that circulated around town after was something that would stick with him for a long time from then on. He got home and told his dad they would not be bothering him every again it was all that needed to be said. His dad was satisfied but his mother was worried, she didn't like violence and she looked at son.

"Are you alright love?" she asked him seeing his eye swelling a little and his lip cut.

"Yes I am fine; how about a cuppa have we got any biscuits"

Max finished up his food and drink then Richard put him back into the vehicle. He walked into the pub and across to where Stephanie was sitting the food had arrived and they both ate.

"You remember this pub?" she asked seeing he was looking round somewhat as he ate.

"It has a few memories my mum and dad used to drink in here actually"

"I see, well I hope they are happy memories" she smiled at him and continued eating he said nothing and ate his food in silence

CHAPTER FIFTEEN

Later that day Richard could see Stephanie was dealing with something she was not telling him. She was quiet and self absorbed. They were walking through town to get a few things and she just seemed to clam up on the way back to the vehicle.

"You going to tell me or are you going to be doing the quiet thing all day?"

"I think you already know and I have made a complete mess of things" she said as they got back to the Land Rover. Richard settled in his seat and turned to face Stephanie as she closed the door and just looked forward.

"It is time, we are now going to come clean and we are now going to decide what to do" Richard said in a calm and composed way.

"I am the beacon Richard, it is homing in on me, it knew you would come for me and it knew I would find you. I have to warn you of the impending danger and I have done that the best I can. But I am so sorry and worried I have had to put you in this danger it knows you can summon or contact someway someone who can destroy it, and it will stop you"

"You have not put me in danger"

"Of course I have, it is because of me it is hunting you down" she turned to him and saw he was looking at her in a blank but calm way.

"Stephanie I am not stupid, a little dense sometimes but not stupid, you have been mixed up and changing your story from the first night. Stop all this silly bugger and let's see what we can do with what we know" he looked her in the eye and she again was looking at the old Richard, the young boy who used to protect her as a child and promised he always would She took a deep breath and held his hand in hers.

"What I said about me being taken is true I tried but fail and was sucked into oblivion, this thing knew my mother was strong, I stupidly broke the spell and I will never forgive myself for it. But my mother knew of a greater force than her own, the only other power strong enough to destroy this evil and you are the key to that power, It wants to finish you Richard finish you once and for all. I am thinking it made a way for me to escape and knew I was predictable enough to take it. I knew it was done on purpose but I had to get out of that horrible place, even if it was only for a short while. It used me to find you and released the blackest vilest thing that lurks..."

"Stephanie I know whatever it is is using you it is obvious they are tracking you because they know I will have you and keep you safe. I figured that out a while ago. That is not the issue what we need to do is find a way to destroy the bloody thing" Richard was calm and it made Stephanie feel calmer as she spoke to him. She needed his logic and his strength because she had been struggling with hers ever since she escaped.

"That is what I have been telling you Richard you can't, it is not something you just kill it is not like anything you have ever come across before" she squeezed his hand and felt the pain in her heart and soul ripping her from the inside out.

"Why have they not sent this thing before, all these years that I have been doing this crap, why now why have they sent it now?"

"There must be a reason but I just do not know why, but I do know it is getting close and I think you would be better off without me. I have told you all I know and what I can tell you. If I leave and go then you will have more time before it finds you" she had worry in her eyes and her hand was squeezing Richard's hard but she was unaware she was doing it.

"Well get that stupid thought out of you head lass, we stick together and there is no argument about that. There is always a way to fight everything one way of another. This darkness or whatever the bloody thing is, it controls other things, people you say?"

"Yes it can turn anything against you, so let's say there was group of ten men over there, she pointed to the distance hypothetically, then it could turn them against you they would just do it and attack you they would not be able to control themselves, and it can do this with almost everyone or anything you don't have a chance Richard. You can't fight everything on the planet, I just don't know what else to do, I used to be so sure and thought I was powerful and wise, it turns out I was weak and stupid, I reversed what my mother did and let it back in"

"The only way to beat pure evil is pure good?" he asked again composed and serene

"Yes that is what I am trying to tell you, it is not a fight you can win, it is a situation where you need help and there is only one person who can do that"

"I have come home to end it and the person who is going have to help is the one person who brought me into this world. The strongest and kindest person I have ever encountered. But I have never felt this help before; it is only now that she comes to light" he said solemnly

"Yes, yes that is it, you must ask for her to help how many more signs do you need Richard, this is it this is the last place and the first place in your life. You were born here and here is where..." she stopped and shook her head.

"Die here?" he finished her sentence for her.

“I didn’t say that, you can escape you can be free and you must take that chance Richard please you must. Don’t let the darkness win. There is no hope for me I am sure of that but there is much hope for you and I have tried so hard to convince you but time is running out. Ask for help, you need her one last time, leave all this behind, you have done enough” she looked at him pleadingly. He squeezed her hand back and smiled at her she shook her head at him and sighed out with a smile she could not hold back.

“These last few days I have remembered things long forgot and locked away. Come back home like you say. My mum was so weak and frail before she died but she still carried on protecting me from the truth and the hurt and pain she was feeling. That is real strength when you are hurting but mask it to protect others. My dad died and I looked after her and tried to help and give her what I could. She always told me, it is better to walk alone than walk with the wrong crowd. She used to pray every night before she went to sleep, but not for herself she prayed for others, for me. Always wanting good for other people, always seeing the good in other people. I have seen much and experienced too much, I have seen evil I know it exists and I know you cannot always trust others, seeing the good doesn’t always work because some just take advantage of good honest people. But her faith was so strong and she was such a fighter and she battled hurt all her life. Arthritis ate away at her and she was in pain all the time with it but she never complained, not once she just got on with it" Richard stopped for a moment and Stephanie could see he was thinking to himself and maybe regretted saying these things because obviously he had never said them to anyone before.

"They do not make them like her any more Richard, it is a different generation, she was a fighter like her son, she was vigilant like her son and she loved her son unconditionally. You owe her this chance to prove to you one last time how much she loved and cared for you. Please do not shut her out it is just wrong. You know she can help, you know this is it and you know deep down you know, she is there waiting for you"

"She knew people well and she did like you, she told me to "stick with her she is a good person" I had plans to do so then you left. My dad moved us back up To Yorkshire after that, but I never forgot you. If this is the time for it to end then so be it. But you are not going back there if I am ending it then so are you"

"Oh Richard I can't go anywhere else I am condemned to eternal pain and torture I only had this one chance to help and save you" she started to fill up and then she cried and pulled into his arm sobbing uncontrollably. He let her sob he knew it was good for her to release it all he put his hand on her head and gently pulled her into him. Holding her he glanced back at Max who was sat up looking at him. They locked eyes and were joined. They often did this and both of them seemed to unite it was a very personal thing between a man and his dog, only this was no ordinary dog and this was no ordinary man.

"There is always a way and if you can't find it then you carry on looking, we have not come this far through this much just to give up Stephanie, you are stronger than that love. Stop letting it, win over you and you will prevail, we are going to find a way and all three of us will succeed in doing so you mark my words lass"

She lifted her head and smiled through her tears she knew it was an impossible situation for her but seeing him look at her and hearing his voice made her calm again. It was something she could not explain and something much deeper than anyone would ever understand but she felt better instantly and sniffed up drying her eyes with her hands.

"You are rather the bravest man ever or a stupid crazy Bastard you know that don't you?"

"Well, I try my best. How long do you think we have?"

"Not long, days maybe less, it is near Richard I can feel its presence approaching I don't know why but I can feel it," she said shrugging her shoulders and sighing out.

"Well we have found our battle ground and it's my home ground so that is to my advantage, you just stay focused and strong and we shall win through this one way or another you will see. Do not; plant doubt in your mind or doubt will grow. Keep believing we will win through and keep the faith in what we can do strong. No matter what happens don't give in to doubt Stephanie. I need you strong I need the girl who is now a woman who pulled me from tarn you threw me I need the girl who was brave and courageous back then I need you" he looked her straight in the eye and she returned the gaze, it was electric and uplifting.

"You got it Richard but remember what I said you can't just fight your way out of this one, it is different it is dangerous and it is like nothing that has confronted you before"

"Well we have help and it is the strongest purest help I know so let's stop talking about it and let's get the job done. It's going to be dark soon and I think we need to find somewhere to bed down for the night. I know of a few places around here and they are out of town and secluded we can recharge and then tomorrow I have a church to visit" Richard said no more and turned forward he started up the Land Rover and drove off. Stephanie sat back in her seat and glanced over at Max. She wondered if he knew if he had any idea what was happening. Looking straight ahead she was pleased Richard had finally come to terms with it all and accepted what she had been trying so hard to tell him. They drove in silence and it was not long before they were parking up in an old courtyard by a farmhouse, passing a sign advertising a vacancy. Somewhere he obviously knew about from way back. He reached into his pocket and pulled out some cash.

"Go in there and book us a room, I have somewhere to go and will be back shortly" He told her and she suddenly felt cold and alone. It was unexpected and she was confused.

"Wait, what, no Let me stay with you please" she insisted in an almost pleading manner.

"You will be safe here I won't be long now the sooner you get in there the sooner I can get back trust me" he looked at her and waited for her to get out of the land Rover. She knew she could not change his mind so she conceded and did as she was told.

Getting out of the Land Rover she felt suddenly alone and turned to watch Richard drive away, her heart sank for a moment and the fear of him not returning crossed her mind. She waited until the Land Rover was gone out of sight then she turned and slowly walked into the main entrance, feeling worried but then again confident it was a mixed emotion.

He drove quickly he headed back to the small church he had been to earlier it didn't take him too long to reach it. The light was fading but it was till light enough. He stopped outside of the road side and turned to Max. He reached over and petted his dog for a moment to reassure him and then got out of the Land Rover and walked towards the small church. He went through a gateway but the small gate was long gone. He could see the grass had over grown the pathway and it was obvious not many people came here anymore.

The memories all came flashing back to him as he turned the black metal round handle and pushed the old wooden squeaking door open. It was just as he remembered it small and old. The stone floor was well worn with hundreds of years of people walking over it and it was more worn in places than others. The single row of benches still down the middle and the place still the same as it was. A giant cross with Jesus Christ nailed to it hung at the front and there was an elevated section where the sermons used to be given. It was chilly and very silent; the history that was within these walls must go back hundreds of years. He sighed out and went to sit in the exact place he remembered sitting all those years ago with his old frail mother. It was when she was ailing and she had asked him to take her here one last time. Sitting down he looked round and his mind shot back to that time.

"Richard you must listen to me" his little mother said grey and weak looking; she held his powerful hand in her bony weak one, distorted with arthritis.

"I always listen to you ma?" Richard said smiling at her.

“I know you do son but I am not going to be around for long, I want to make sure you are going to be safe when I am gone” she looked into his face and he looked back at her old face that was so wise and so kind”

“You will be fine ma, you are going to be around for some time yet” He told her smiling.

“Oh no, I have had enough, but please listen to me, I have come to this special place all my life and this one last time I thank you for bringing me here” she looked round the small church and had a moment with her thoughts she touched the silver crucifix around her neck hanging down with a small thing chain.

“Don’t talk like that, ma, you are going to be ok lass”

“When your dad died, you helped me a lot and I really appreciate that, it was not easy when he got ill and I had to look after him. He was not always an easy man to live you. But he was a good man deep down; he was a worker and a provider”

“Yes he was, I miss him ma”

“So do I son so do I, he was a pain in the arse at times but I miss the old bugger” she smiled a dry smile and squeezed Richards hand but there was not much power in her weak grip.

“He will be looking down on us and saying we are silly buggers you know that”

"Well yeah I am sure, but I am worried for you Richard, please promise me you will look after yourself, and please promise me you will stay safe" she pulled his hand towards her and she held it close to her as she looked up at him.

"I will always try ma, I promise you that"

"I will always be watching you and you only have to ask me for help if you ever need it son, please never forget that" she leaned forward and Richard did the same they gently touched heads and Richard smiled at her and she smiled back at him

"Thank you ma, you are the strongest woman I have ever known, probably ever will know, I promise you I will not go off the rails"

"Better to walk your way alone than the wrong way with the crowd" she softly said.

"I don't like crowds you know that"

"You are a loner I know but it is a bad dark world out there, you must stay safe for me you must believe Richard, have faith son, please have faith"

"Mum I will take on anything that comes my way, you are not going anywhere you are a strong woman and have many more years left in you yet you old bugger" he smiled at her and again she smiled back at him but he could see the hurt and pain in her eyes. She had had enough and knew it was about time. It saddened

Richard to see it but he didn't show it and stayed strong in front of her, a sense of pride and admiration rising within him.

"You need to get a woman you need to settle down get yourself a good woman son"

"I will try and see what's out there" he smiled at her making light humour of it

"I am serious, someone to look after you"

"I can look after myself ma, don't worry all will be fine" he straightened up and they both sat up right looking forward to the front.

"Jesus died on that cross to save us all, I feel you have a journey to take and you will save people Richard, I have a feeling you have a long and hard path to walk son"

"Better I don't get a woman then eh?" he regretted joking when he saw his mother praying as she looked up at the large Cross at the front of the church. He noticed how frail she had become and it pained him to see it, she used to be so strong and to think she used to carry him on her shoulders down the back field. How things change and how old age affects everyone he thought. Life is cruel offering you so much but giving you so little time to enjoy it all.

He let her finish and gave her respected silence, she eventually turned to him and smiled squeezing his hand again she looked into his eyes.

“I had you very late in life, you were so tiny when you were born, you were premature by a few weeks, the nurse brought you to me and I said I was worried you were so small, and she told me not to worry because you have all the time in the world to grow. And she said be kind to them and show them love and they will do the same to you when you get older. And here you are big and strong and looking after me, thank you Richard for being a wonderful son” she took a deep breath and sighed out slowly as she looked at him lovingly and admiringly.

“It is in my genes ma, what I am is all because of you darling, you are my strength my power and my armour, you have devoted your life to us and I am eternally grateful to you. The best mum in the world and don’t you ever forget that” He gently squeezed her hand and she smiled up at him, love and kindness in her eyes.

“Thank you son, thank you so much, your dad helped a lot too”

“You were the best parents I could of ever wished for, I always had food and shelter I was always shown love and compassion I was taught right from wrong and how to appreciate and you were both always by my side and on my said, the only ones who had my back. The only ones I could truly trust, so no, thank you ma thank you so much” he leaned forward and gently kissed her head and she smiled wide at him.

"You are going to make me cry in a minute" she told him dropping her head into his shoulder and resting it there.

"It is true ma you are a very special woman, very special indeed"

"And you are a very special son my Richard"

They stayed like for a few minutes saying nothing and just being quiet, eventually His mother raised her head and looked round the church slowly.

"You ok?" He asked her noticing her frail look and grey hair suddenly more.

"Yes I remember when there used to be a lot of people in here, when I was in the children's home the nuns who brought us up were very strict, we used to come here every Sunday and you did as you were told back then or you were punished. It would be classed as cruelty if they did it now a days. But it taught you discipline and respect. Something that is lacking in this world now I feel" she sighed and turned to look at her son once again.

"I agree with you and it's getting worse, society is to free and easy they don't need to work for anything anymore so don't appreciate anything annoying really"

"Thank you for bringing me here today"

"I will take you anywhere at any time ma you know that"

"I know you will you are a good boy, you always have been we have always been close, but if you ever forget me later in life, always remember I am here son, I am always here"

"I will never forget you ma, you are imprinted on my very soul"

"I will never forget you either son, you are my pride and joy and my whole life"

The memories flooded back and Richard stood up, he looked about the small church again and then sat down looking at the seat his little ma sat in all those years ago. He had never cried in his adult life but he felt a lump in his throat. His life had been for this one moment to bring him back home to reunite him with the one person who had always been with him but he had not called upon. His eyes filled up with tears and he didn't fight it. All the years of fighting all the years of pain, all the things he had seen seem to bring him here, he can't go on forever. A light that had been there all his life he just had not seen it, or realised. He took out the small crucifix and held it in his hand it felt warm and he opened his hand looking at it resting in his palm. He sniffed up and let his tears fall into his hand and they hit the crucifix as they did. Tears that were his first and tears that were filled with all his power and all his strength, they were the rarest of things in his life and now he gave them freely.

“I need your help mother, I need your help” Has he said the words the crucifix moved it was very slight but it moved and he watched has slowly but surely it began to get brighter in his hand. The small cross shone bright like a small beacon then it faded once again. He looked up to the front of the church it was silent and still he looked round and could sense something but it was not bad, it was something he had never felt before. Comforting and calming it seemed to encase him like an invisible hug. Then suddenly it was gone, he spun around on his heels and searched with his eyes the entire place but it was empty and quiet. He felt something, something so strong in that moment. He put the crucifix back in his pocket and wiped his eyes. He smiled and took a deep breath, things seemed to make sense all of a sudden, his destiny maybe his quest whatever it was it was here. He was home and it felt good to him, it felt safe and it felt secure. He left the church a happier and more content man but he still knew he had a job to do.

CHAPTER SIXTEEN

Stephanie had been thinking a lot and realised she had been used; it must have read her thoughts or her mind and found out about Richard and his Mother's power. Feeling somewhat ashamed of herself she sighed and lay curled up on the bed. Closing her eyes she saw her mother's soul there encasing the evil. She saw herself chanting and thinking she was powerful enough but she was nowhere near it. The darkness engulfed her and took her down into the darkness she heard her mother scream she felt her head explode from within all her fears all her thoughts were dragged from her skull it knew everything she knew. The spell had been broken by her coming to this place. Her mistake had released the evil from her mother's grip and encased her in the blackness of torment. She was allowed to escape to find Richard so this thing could destroy him and then nothing would be left to summon the one person who was its enemy and nemesis. It made her sob and sad that she had caused so much sorrow and been so stupid to think she was powerful enough to defeat this. Not knowing how long she had been there she heard the Land Rover pull up outside, and she was so pleased when he finally walked in to the room she had been on edge all the time he had been gone. Max trotted in and lay down by the bottom of the bed Stephanie came over to meet Richard as he came through the door.

"Where have you been, are you alright I was getting worried" she said to him

"Enlightened you could say" he smiled at her and went over to the small table and flicked the kettle on to make himself some tea, he started to search the complimentary biscuits and then decided to take them all.

"Where did you go?" she followed him to the small table side where the kettle was.

"Is this the only bloody biscuits they have? Stingy swine's" he complained

"Richard, answer me" she took him by the shoulders and pulled him around to face her.

"I went on a journey and have come back a better man"

"Where did you go" she asked again slowly and deliberately losing patience

"I had something I had to do and now I have done it, stop pestering we have plans to make and things to work out"

"You are infuriating at times" she said frustrated.

"Yeah well it took me years to perfect it"

"We were lucky to get this room there is a big football match on tomorrow or the day after and they are expecting a lot of supporters to hit town and the pubs, this one included"

"Bloody football, nothing but aresholes kicking a bladder of air about a field for ridiculous money and the moronic trouble causers that follow them around"

"We need to stay clear of them and we need to know what we are doing, time is running out, we can't just keep running there is nowhere to go you must make a decision"

"I know and we must find a way to make you safe" he took the kettle and made a cup of tea and took this with the biscuits to the bed, he sat on it and put the tea and biscuits on the little side table. He looked over at Max who had settled at the bottom of the bed and then he looked at Stephanie who was still stood in the same spot looking at him wide eyed.

"Have you listened to what I have told you Richard, this is so painful and frightening for me I have tried to hold it all together but I know what is coming I know it is near and I am scared" She began to shake and he gestured her to join him, she came over and sat next to him on the bed. He put his arm around her and she leaned into him.

“I felt something tonight I have never felt in my entire life, and now I have no fear of what is coming and I have no fear of what might happen” he took a sip of his tea.

“What do you mean, she asked not moving from her position, you fear nothing anyway, you never have fearless is your middle name?”

“I had a fear deep inside me, I locked it away but tonight that fear is now gone it’s been lifted away. All the years struggle and fighting brought me here to this place at this time, back home that is why I am here Stephanie” he dunked a biscuit in his tea and ate it.

“I am not sure what you mean, I do not understand, what fear did you have what happened tonight Richard, please tell me” she lifted her head and faced him.

“I went back in time and found what I was looking for, I was always too busy looking forward when the answer was behind me, somewhere in my past somewhere locked away in my mind and all I needed was to release it but I never knew how. But now I do and I have and I now understand” he smiled slightly at her.

“You are talking in riddles, you are not making sense to me” she frowned in confusion and tried to read his face but he was not giving anything away.

"My Mum and Dad had me very late in life, I was not planned and it must have been hard for them. I was growing up they were growing old and you don't always realise it. They both suffered with their health dad with his breathing and mum with her Arthritis. When my dad was ill my mum looked after him and when he died it took a lot out of her she seemed to age very quickly. But you don't realise until it is too late. What they gave up for you and what sacrifices they made. One moment they are big and strong to you then before you know it they are old and weak and grey. But it is the spirit that stays strong and that is what keeps them going. I realised tonight just how strong that spirit was, how strong it is. Whatever happens, Stephanie you always remember that, remember the spirit is strong and carries on"

"I will try" was all she could say she didn't understand what he was saying but she could see now that something had moved him and she hoped it was what she thought it was.

"The problem is you are fighting bad, the darkness all the time when the real power I need is in the light, we must destroy this darkness Stephanie and once we do the light will always be there, always shine through and will always be all powerful, I think she knew I would be back one day I think she was a very wise lady and very strong woman"

"Yes, but please you need to understand, we are running out of time it is near I know it is so near, I am at a loss what to do now, I don't know..." she sighed out and shook her head.

He could see her panic and frustration and tried to inject a little humour.

"Is it because I have taken all the biscuits and you have no tea?" he held a straight face but she didn't find it funny she looked at him and wondered if her really understood, if he ever really understood or he just took everything head on and hoped for the best.

"Where did you go tonight and what happened?" she said as calm as she could still looking at him with desperation in her eyes, backed up with determination to get an answer.

"I went back and realised something, I went back to a time when I had a guardian angel and didn't realise I still do, I only had to ask" he smiled at her and she eventually smiled back at him realising finally what he meant and was trying to say.

"You saw her?" she gasped relived and pleased

"No but she was there, thank you for making me realise my fate after all and thank you for what you have done, but this fight is mine now and you must get safe"

"I can't I am doomed I told you that" she dropped her head again and held back the tears.

"I don't believe it, there is always a way and we will find it, if we defeat this thing then it has no hold over you, no more power over you, we will get you safe Stephanie" he took a long drink of his tea and ate a biscuit she looked at him and shook her head. He was actually drinking tea and eating biscuits at a time like this when she was barely holding it together. She didn't know whether to punch him hug him or kiss him, or just take the bloody biscuits off him or all three.

"You are so bloody infuriating at times Richard Cushing"

"It's called a gift" he smiled slightly at her and she had no choice but to smile back at him.

"Make me a tea and shut the hell up" she said and stood to go to the bathroom. Richard just lay out on the bed and stretched for a moment then he got up and walked over to Max and sat with him on the floor. Max wagged his tail once and looked at his Master. Richard put his head on his dogs and put his hands around the dog's neck. He hugged him and they lay together for a while. Nothing else had to be done it was a bonding only they understood. Stephanie came back into the room and clicked her tongue she went and made her own tea while Richard and his dog lay on the floor. She reached over and stole the biscuits Richard had left on the side she made her tea and sat down on the bed with her own thoughts.

"We need fuel, will fill up in town tomorrow and then get you safe somewhere lass" Richard eventually said still laid on the floor next to Max.

"Safe, where is that place? Because I have no idea" she answered him worried and confused why he thought she could be saved, she knew and felt she could not.

"You will never find a rainbow if you are always looking down"

"Accept what is, let go of what was, have faith in what will be?" she added

"There you go, you are on the right track now lass" Richard stood up and looked for his biscuits but was disappointed when he noticed Stephanie had already eaten them. She looked at him with a little smile and took a sip of her tea.

"Thank you, you always seem to calm me, you always have" she told him he took the cup of tea he had and finished it taking it to the side.

"I am getting a shave and shower" he then disappeared into the bathroom. Stephanie put her cup down on the side table and lay out on the bed she looked up at the ceiling and clasped her hands behind her head. She remembered the time she met Richard's mother, how tiny she seemed and fragile in stature but so strong in character and spirit. It made her smile remembering her and how

Richard looked after her. Thinking how Richard had turned out and what she already knew at the time. How different it would be if circumstances had been altered. His spirit is to strong and untamed. Whatever happens she was thankful for the time she spent with this man and thankful for the life she had here and beyond. It was a full and eventful and rewarding experience. Clinging to the hope that Richard somehow could save her from her fate was welcoming but she could not see how it could be. What she experienced and suffered in that depth of darkness made her shiver and the thought of going back there made her panic and gasp. Maybe he could save her, maybe there was a way, she had to keep this thought alive and stay focused. Whatever happens she must do her best and try, at the very least she must try. Closing her eyes the sleep started to creep in and she felt tired. Worry and stress had taken its toll and her body and mind demanded rest. She never heard Richard come back into the room and she didn't notice he lay on the floor with Max for the longest time. She stirred when she heard him rummaging in his bag; she looked at him as he turned to look back at her. He was just wearing bottoms and nothing else.

He came to the bed and lay next to her, taking her hand he placed something in it and closed her fingers around it. He then planted a gentle kiss on her lips. Her heart jumped and she opened her hand to see what he had placed there. Tears came to her eyes as she saw the small stone shaped as a heart. The same one she gave him when they were ten years old the same stone he said he would keep and give back to her when they were grown up and together.

She looked into his eyes and melted, this was something so special she could not hold back her emotions, she remembered this stone from time to time but it had not recently.

"You kept it, kept it all this time" she said looking into his blue eyes.

"Of course I kept it, that is my most prized possession a very special girl gave me that, and I promised to look after it and return it one day"

"You always keep your promises Richard Cushing" she smiled and put her face close to his and their heads touched.

"Well I try my best, she was a very unique girl" he smiled at her and she could feel his breath on her face and she started to breathe heavier herself.

"Is this were we are suppose to fall into bed and make mad passionate love and ride off into the sunset together?" she said almost in a whisper.

"I don't know, will you be gentle with me" he smiled

"Can't promise it but I will try" they kisses deeply and made love, forgetting all what had happened all that could happen it didn't matter, not in that moment which was a monumental event in their lives, it was their destiny it was what they both had been wanting and now the special bond they always had would be stronger than ever, they were now joined, spiritually and physically forever as one.

CHAPTER SEVENTEEN

Richard was outside with Max when Stephanie awoke; she yawned and looked round getting her bearings. Surprisingly she had slept deeply and soundly she felt much better for it and just for this short time had forgotten about the dilemma and danger she was in. Rolling over she stretched out and then shook her head and got off the bed. Realising Richard and Max were gone she panicked for a moment and dashed to the window, looking out she sighed in relief as she saw them both walking back towards the room. Turning back she went into the toilet and then heard them come in.

"Good morning" she shouted from her seated position.

"Let's hope so, but the morning is almost over you have been sleeping for hours, it is past eleven, we have missed breakfast already" Richard's voice came back from the bed room. He had already packed the bag and it was just a matter of when Stephanie was ready so they could leave.

"Oh I am sorry I didn't know, I will be right out"

"No rush we can get something in town I have to fill up with fuel anyway then we get you away safe and we finish this lass" his voice was confident and she felt more secure it was so.

Max had already been fed and watered and been out for a long walk so he was happy. Stephanie got a quick shower and was ready soon after. She came back in and looked at them both sat together on the bed they both turned their heads and looked at her as she came in.

“I’m done I am ready” she said with a little smile.

“I have already packed up and paid the bill so let’s get out of here and get the day started”

They all left and she had no idea what they were going to do or where they were going to go. But strangely it didn’t bother her like before she could see the confidence in him and she trusted that without question. They drove away in silence and the day was becoming cloudy. Max sat up on the back and Stephanie in the front. Richard drove the land Rover fast and headed for town he needed to fill the vehicle up with diesel then head away. He noticed St George’s flags out of windows and in houses. He clicked his tongue and shook his head. He then saw a group of men marching off down the street shouting and chanting some football song. Stephanie looked at them and didn’t like it; she never liked loud men and especially drunk loud men. Richard headed for the petrol station in town he got there and drove up to the pump. Getting out he noticed some more men all dressed in football supporters gear heading for a pub. He looked away saying nothing. When he finally got the Land Rover full of diesel he went in to pay. Going to the glass protected desk he stood waiting for the man on the other side it to stop looking at the TV behind him, Richard lost patience instantly.

"Today would be good" he said loudly.

"Oh Sorry mate, just seeing the final line up you watching the match at home or in the pub?" the man said as he looked at how much Richard owed.

"What are you on about?" Richard asked him.

"The bloody match, big day, judgment day world cup man, England in the final" The man looked shocked and was totally surprised Richard had to ask.

"Sounds lovely can we hurry up I am already late" Richard said uninterested. The man pressed a button and Richard paid with his credit card at the card machine.

"You want your receipt?" the man asked with a dirty look and hostile voice. Richard would have normally fired back but was not in the mood.

"No, you keep it to dry your tears when we lose"

"Prick" the man said under his breath as Richard left and went back to the Land Rover.

"Everything alright?" Stephanie asked seeing him shaking his head.

"Bloody world cup is on, the pubs will be packed with knob heads and when we lose they will go on a riot they always do, fucking brainless buggers, should have known with all the bloody flags everywhere"

"Oh shit let's get out of here please" She didn't like the sound of it and looked round and noticed many men and woman walking about some already drunk others holding cans of beer, wearing scarf's and footballs shirts and the whole place was alive with them.

Richard started up the Land Rover but suddenly was blocked by a coach full of shouting and cheering men. The driver had pulled in to fill up and had blocked Richard's exit.

"Fucking idiot" Richard shouted but Stephanie pulled at his arm to calm him down, she didn't need any confrontation right now and was becoming nervous at how many people suddenly seemed to be about, the crowds were gathering and it was making her uneasy.

"Just let them get what they need and they will be gone keep calm please"

"Make me bloody sick they are like brainless zombies shouting and cheering, wandering about like lobotomised sheep" He hit the horn in the middle of his steering wheel but the driver just put his hand up and ignored him. Then he carried on filling the coach up with diesel. Three motorbikes raced past to fast and to loud which also annoyed Richard and he let out a long sigh. Stephanie body had frozen, and her blood had run cold, she began to breathe erratically and she locked her door securely. He glanced over to her noticing the fear on her face and the tremble in her hands, blood had drained from her cheeks.

"What is it, what's wrong?" he said and looked to where she was staring with open eyes. Ahead of them coming down the small field was a fog like blackness, much easier to see now in daylight rolling down the hillside and moving un-naturally into town, it was the darkness it had found them and it was heading straight for them.

Without hesitation He backed up he spun the Land Rover around and knocked over a waste bin, the men on the coach started to shout and holler at him and the man in the garage was pointing and shouting too. Richard locked his own door then turned his vehicle around and did a three point turn he headed out of the petrol station wrong way up a one way system. Stephanie looked back and saw the Darkness expanding it was like a growing entity covering the place like a drifting smoke and now it was touching people, men woman and children it was passing over and around them. She could see them change she could see the difference instantly. It was moving fast it was gaining and she suddenly had all her fear back. Richard put his foot down and raced off out of the petrol station but he was going the wrong way and had to head out into traffic, he turned and hit a parked car, his large powerful Land Rover with its bull bar was always going to win that confrontation. The car was shunted out of the way and he turned into the traffic but it was slowing and the darkness was moving towards them fast. He reversed again and turned the wheel they were thrown to the side but he managed to get going up the road. Max lay down and held on the best he could Stephanie fastened her seat belt and put her trust in Richard, she had no other choice she tried to hide her fear but it was not easy. The darkness was effecting everyone it touched and they all mindlessly seemed to obey they started to run and chant and cheer after the Land Rover. They had one thing on their minds and that was to destroy that Vehicle and all who were in it. Soon it was a raging mob and more and more joined as the darkness quickly moved and expanded over the whole town. The coach had raced from the petrol station and was giving chase already the men in it shouting and screaming after the Land Rover. Suddenly something had been thrown at them and Stephanie ducked, then more things came from all sides, stones, beer cans, dustbins, whatever was in reach the people on the side of the road picked up and threw what they could at the moving Land Rover. Richard was pleased he was in this vehicle it was strong and robust and could take a lot of punishment the items tended to just bounce off. The bull bars on the front served a good battering ram and he was going to use it as and when he needed. This was a drive of survival he could not afford to stop or be boxed in. Max started to growl and Richard gritted his teeth as he fought to keep control. Two motorbikes caught him up and came along the side. Both riders shouting obscenities at him, he turned his wheel and knocked one off and he veered up the kerb and through a shop window landing awkwardly and being trapped under his bike. The second bike raced off in front, suddenly they were shunted from the back the coach full of supporters had rammed into the back of them, Dropping a gear Richard put his foot down and gained some distance but had to slow because of the junction ahead, there was a stopped car at it but Richard just went forward and rammed it from behind and out of the way violently and quickly he turned and headed off up the road.

The coach had to slow and stop it could not make the same manoeuvre but it eventually got around the junction and again gave chase. The streets were becoming full and people seemed to be coming from everywhere. The darkness was engulfing the whole town and they were all on the rampage to get to them but they didn't really know why they just felt compelled to do so. Two men suddenly landed of the roof of the Land Rover, Richard had no idea from where, he slammed on his breaks and skidded to a stop. Instantly the men were thrown off and landed nastily on the ground before him. Without a second thought he just carried on and knocked them both out of the way hitting them with the bull bar he had no worry in doing so and had no care what happened to them. The road was becoming crowded with people there was no other option but to just plough through them. Stephanie covered her eyes and screamed as angry faces appeared at the windows and tried to open the doors.

"Hold on" Richard shouted and put his foot down. He had no choice he could not stop, they were grabbing at his Land Rover it was being rocked from side to side and men were thumbing and kicking at it. He drove hard and knocked many out of the way he felt the wheels run over something but carried on. The Land Rover was kicked and things were thrown at it from all sides. It was mayhem and madness, chaos and violence, they were driven by an invisible evil that they had no control over, all they wanted to do was kill and destroy. It was a frenzied attack and more and more people were joining from the side streets and pubs, shops everywhere. The expanding darkness was all around and covering everything in sight, it was like a dark fog corrupting everything it touched. Max was barking and snarling at the faces appearing at the windows and trying to smash their way in. Stephanie had covered her faced with her hands and was shaking it was a terrifying ordeal and she had to bite her lip hard to stop screaming. Suddenly

Richard turned the vehicle to the left then to the right and did this over and over as he went down the street. It knocked people off and out of the way. He suddenly turned into a supermarkets entrance he had some space and used it by racing away over the large car park. The mob was running after him screaming and shouting. Two cars started to race from the side and were going to Ram him but he managed to speed past and one over shot and hit the kerb bouncing the car up and damaging the front wheel, while the other turned quickly and gave chase.

"Fucking wankers" he cursed and headed for the far exit speeding out he almost lost control and had to fight to regain it, he had the Land Rover up on two wheels and pulled the steering wheel round to try and right it. The wheels came bouncing back down bouncing them from their seats and they were again racing away down the road. Max was thrown off the seat but got back and did he manage to secure himself somehow digging his claws in to the seat. Richard was intense and driving hard and fast it was a hunt and he was the hunted but no way would he give up without a fight.

Looking back Stephanie could see men shouting and cursing at them giving chase, she then suddenly felt a violent and powerful jolt to her side as the coach from earlier rammed into them from a side street. She screamed and was violently knocked to the side her seat belt tightening to pull her back.

Fighting hard to keep control Richard did all he could to keep it going, he managed it but he was lucky in doing so. Then suddenly a man was stood in front of them in the road clenching his fists and the veins in his neck standing out with the strain he had snarling his face at them. Not giving it a second thought and just kept going and knocked the man off to the side, he was that drunk the man just got up and started to run after them, oblivious to anything.

The whole town now was infected with this darkness of evil they were racing towards the Land Rover from all sides from all angles. Cars vans bikes and coaches all started to head in the same direction drawn by some un-earthy presence that they didn't understand or could control they were driven and guided blindly. Hundreds of people running towards the same target, the darkness driving them on making them do as it willed. They had no choice and could not resist this entity force that was controlling their will and actions.

They were gaining a bit of distance and heading out of town, but their luck was short lived he saw ahead of him coming down the road a large Truck. Much bigger than him much more powerful and he knew if this hit him he was done for. The large Truck speeded up and the tonnage of metal and roaring engine of this beast was racing towards him hitting parked cars and knocking them to the side as if they were little toys tossing them up onto the pavement. The driver shouting some obscenities as he did so, his gaze was focused on the Land Rover in front of him. Richard had no choice he had to turn off luckily there was a side street but he had to make a quick turn and the truck sped past missing him by only inches. He heard it coming to a screeching halt and reversing. Wasting no time he put his foot down and raced on he was now going in the wrong direction but at least he was going. This was his home town so he knew it well and it was a good job he did, it was going to be fatal to get boxed in somewhere and he had to get out of town quickly. They could hear the shouting and roar of the hundreds of voices screaming and raging all over the town. Stephanie found it very un-nerving and was panicking looking in all directions out of the windows as they raced along. Every now and then something hit the Land Rover that had been thrown from a house window or from the side of the road. Nothing was going to deflect Richard's attention though he knew he had to get out of town and away from this population. Slowing down he turned out of the street and along the road next to the leisure park area. Men were running across the grass towards him but he easily out ran them and headed over the small roundabout and then right again towards the main road. He now was heading in the right direction again. A motorbike suddenly appeared in his rear view mirror then another and some more until there were six bikes following him. He hated bikers at the best of times so this didn't make him happy at all. They call caught up and were directly behind him. He kept an eye on them through his rear view and side mirrors.

He knew they were trying to box him in but didn't know how to go about it. Looking forward he saw two smaller cars racing along in front of him.

"Hold on and stay focused" Richard said then rammed on his breaks, bringing the Land Rover to a sudden stop two bikers were not quick enough and awkwardly and painfully rammed into the back of him. The others swerved around and over shot in front of him. Speeding back up, he then went for them and hit two again with the front of his Vehicle sending one off to the side the rider flying from his bike and crashing into the pavement and the other one under his wheels. The Land Rover bounced and rolled over the bike and was soon back on its way. The two remaining bikers had stopped up the road and were looking back at him. Black helmets on and dark visors pulled down so you could not see their faces. But there were shouting and yelling at the oncoming Land Rover they both then revved their machines and sped off into the distance. The two small cars were racing with them and Richard opened up the speed on his Land Rover he had a chance here to make some distance. Police sirens could be heard ringing in the distance but they were not here to help they were here to join the man hunt.

Stephanie could hear the thunderous voices of hundreds of men and woman shouting and chanting from what seemed everywhere. Then suddenly she screamed at the sight that confronted her. There must have been hundreds of men marching down the road in front of them. The whole road was full and others were spilled out onto the pavement it was a mass body of people and an army of controlled soldiers. The darkness was hovering above them and it was a horrifying sight her blood ran cold and she began to shake with fear. The noise of them shouting and the roar that came from them as they saw the Land Rover stabbed directly at her heart she was petrified in that moment. The two cars and bikes were gone all she could see now was a mass of aggressive Man starting to charge at them screaming as they did.

Stopping suddenly he put his vehicle in reverse and looked back over his shoulder he put his foot down and raced on, the engine roaring and not liking it going this fast in reverse. He slowed up then pulled his steering wheel down turning the Vehicle sharply and violently around then he put it in forward gear and raced away back the way he had come, the crowd giving chase on foot seemed insane and determined to kill and rip them apart. Racing away Richard stayed focused and kept an eagle eye on the road and area in front of him he did not want to be boxed in or crash now or they were done for. He upped a gear and put his foot down the engine roared and Land Rover took them alone the road.

Knocking a car out of the way as he rammed into it and bounced it off to the side he noticed up ahead the coach again. Cursing he turned off and down a small street luckily it seemed quieter but not for long. It had speed bumps in the road and he just raced over them bouncing everyone about inside he reached the end when he was pelted with missiles and bricks from both sides. His windows cracked but didn't break, bricks bounced off the bonnet and roof. He saw it was about a dozen children cursing at him and throwing everything they had to try and stop him. It looked like the whole town had been taken over and he knew he had to get out, and quickly, it was not going to be easy.

"Listen, no argument Stephanie when we get out of town I want you to get out and run safe, it is me they are following this Land Rover. They won't know you are gone"

"No way Richard, no bloody way, that's stupid I am not leaving you or this Land Rover so you can just forget it" she said adamantly shaking her head.

"It is over Stephanie this is the end, do not give me any bloody argument, there is no use in both of us going down, once they have what they want it will be gone, it is me they are after the Darkness is here for me, you can get free and safe" he insisted without looking at her.

"Richard where and what can I do, they will get you then come looking for me?"

"I will drive them away from you" he said glancing over at her quickly.

"No, if we go we go together, so shut up and drive"

Cursing he didn't give her any argument he just drove up the hill and noticed the cars chasing in his rear view mirror. The chants could still be heard from the angry mob and they were running fast after him. Insanely chasing him and being driven on by the power of the darkness they seemed not to tire or yield. Turning off the road he headed down a dirt track and then off across a field. The Land Rover handled it well but the two cars that were following could not make the transition from road to field and they slowed and were ditched.

"Where are we heading Richard where are you going?" Stephanie asked looking behind and then in front not knowing where she was.

"For help, I hope, it is the only chance we have" was all he said and she then suddenly knew, she looked over at him and saw the determination on his face and it lifted her own spirits.

"Fucking horse" Richard shouted as the large powerful beast was racing from the opposite field its powerful body galloping along and towards them.

"Shit" Stephanie said looking at the charging animal racing for them. It jumped majestically and easily over the stone wall and headed straight for them. The large and powerful animal moved fast and Richard put his foot down to try and get away. Snorting it ran and was staring as it ran at the Land Rover it was gaining more and more distance each second.

"Hold on" he said not wanting to do this but he had no choice. He turned the wheel just at the right time and hit the horse to the side as he brought the Land Rover around and they collided. The beast hit the side of the Land Rover knocking it violently to the side but then bounced off its self. Unsteady it blindly and relentlessly turned and kicked out with its powerful hind legs. Hitting the back end of the land Rover dinting in the metal but not doing much else, Richard had already put his vehicle in reverse. He looked back and rammed into the horse as it turned to face him knocking it violently and painfully down. The horse neighed and lifted its head but could not stand back up. One of its legs was snapped and it just struggled insanely on the floor trying to stand but falling back down, it was finished.

Richard then noticed the tractor it was a big large wheeled kind, an implement carrier, but it had nothing attached. The cab was enclosed and the drivers shouting out like a mad man inside. It was coming fast towards them. The field was relatively flat now so Richard was making good time and distance but the tractor was racing even faster and soon was upon him. It rammed into the side like a rhino and knocked them up for a moment then back down Richard struggled to keep control. The powerful Tractor spun around and came back towards them. Richard braked and managed to make it over shoot missing them. Looking over he saw several men running up the next field with shovels in their hands.

He reversed and quickly and hit the Tractor just as it was turning he rammed it and jolted everyone inside. The tractor was not really moved and took the impact without worry. The large wheels at the back and strong ones at the front acted like shields and Richard knew he was not going to win in any confrontation. Racing forward again he headed for the gate and out onto the road he felt he would have a better chance to out run it on the road. The tractor gave chase and was gaining; it was bouncing up and down on its large tires and taking everything in its stride easily. The rough ground didn't stop or hinder it in any way. Crashing through the gate Richard put his foot down and raced along the road again.

The tractor gave chase roaring like a large animal but as Richard hoped he was able to out run it on the road.

The whole town had come together in uproar of violence and a lynch mob. They were all marching or running towards where Richard was going. He knew it was only a matter of time before they trapped him or caught him off guard. Anyone any time could ram his vehicle or burst his tires and once they were stopped or crashed they would be no chance for them at all.

He had to now put his faith in another power, another being he had to take the chance it was going to work because he was tired of running and had no other choice.

He glanced back at Max then over at Stephanie then he looked forward and headed for the small church, the same one he had been to the night before and hoped he was right.

Stephanie seemed to know she didn't understand why, but she just knew where they were going after that look he had just given her. She knew it was going to be over very soon and she prayed and hoped it would turn out alright for them. She closed her eyes and said a short prayer. This was what she had come back for what she had fought out of hell its self for. This one moment when Richard realised he need that help. That help he had never asked for before but was always there for him. In a way Stephanie was relived but it was a strange relief her fate was unknown and she held out no hope for herself. She was all hope for him though this was a monumental time and a long time coming. She just prayed, hoped and willed this one moment would work this one and only time he would take help and accept what was in front of him. It was his only chance, the one and only chance he had; he must take it or be doomed for eternity. All she could do now was wait and hope she felt her heart beat increasing and her palms sweat but she felt good. It was a very strange feeling but she felt good at this moment.

Richard raced on and he was now focused and the determination could be seen in his face and actions. Max was holding on but not understanding, he wanted to get out and fight but knew if his master was racing away then there must be a good reason. He knew this was the time and he knew all his past battles and fights were down to this one moment in time. Make or break had come, finally after all these years this was it, and no matter what he was going to give it his utmost and fight until the very end.

CHAPTER EIGHTEEN

The church was quiet, sat alone and stood like a monument to another time. It was silent all around it, un-naturally silent. No birds were singing, no noise at all. It seemed like time had slowed down at this very spot. Nothing seemed special about this place but if you were connected, if you were chosen and if you had faith then it was the most powerful place there was, this was the one place Richard was heading for, his only chance and last chance.

Then suddenly the serenity was shattered, in the distance there was sounds of men cheering and chanting and shouting, it was like a ghostly sound at first echoing rolling over the hills but then it started to get louder and stronger. The mob was descending onto this small place. The Land Rover was ahead of them but not by much, Richard raced down the small road and to the front of the church. He stopped and looked at Stephanie who smiled and was amazingly calm, nodded her head and looked over at the church. Taking the small crucifix from his pocket he held it in the palm of his hand. It was shaking slightly and a small glow started to appear all around it.

"Go, fast" he shouted and they all got out of the Land Rover and headed for the church, but suddenly out of ne where something hit Stephanie on the head. She fell and rolled about her hands on the gash that had been caused from the missile. Then another came someone was throwing bricks and stones at them. Max barked and ran forward taking down a man who was coming from behind the church. Richard dodged another brick and ran to help a dazed Stephanie. The noise from the mob was getting louder and getting closer they didn't have much time. A man came dashing forward out of nowhere and attacked Richard, they rolled about on the ground and the man fought like a lunatic hitting biting and scratching. Stephanie stood up and picked up the brick that had been thrown and hit the man hard over the head with it splitting the skull open. But it didn't stop this man he continued to pound punches at Richard. Reaching up Richard grabbed the man's wind pipe with his left hand and twisted his grip, the man could not breath and then Richard pounded his fist into the man's jaw and face knocking him out cold. He pushed the man off to the side and Stephanie helped him to his feet, Looking over they saw Max trotting back after incapacitating his victim.

The noise of the mob grew louder and louder they were running and getting closer, over a hundred human beings charging with hate and evil within them. They all ran to the church's front door. Pushing the wooden door open Richard looked back and could see the mob had caught them up they were charging down the road and violently cursing and shouting at them, this was it was this the end, had the darkness had won.

Suddenly there was a whip crack of noise. It was like nothing any of them had heard before. It was that loud they had to cover their ears with their hands and Max yelped with the pain it caused him. The whole earth seemed to shudder and shake with the tremendous power of it.

The small church had a light within; it was bright shining light that seemed to be part of the church its self. Another loud and devastating ear piercing crack of noise shook the earth and a blinding light followed it. Dazzling everyone and the darkness seemed to stop abruptly, like an invisible force holding it back. The angry mob all fell to their knees holding their ears.

Stephanie looked back and could see something very powerful something so strong that it was holding the darkness at bay, a force and power she had never experienced before.

She never thought it possible but it was being done in front of her eyes. They went into the church and closed the door. Suddenly there was silence, peace and serenity. It was like walking into another world leaving the evil outside.

Walking slowly forward Richard could see the two figures in front of him one was his Father who was stood just behind his Mother. They both smiled at him and looked like they did when they were in their thirties, in their prime, fit and healthy. Richard stood looking at them both and he smiled he knew, he felt it in his heart and he knew. He reached down and touched Max who was staring straight ahead also.

Taking the crucifix he held it out to her and she took a step forward and took it from him. The light intensified and Richard walked forward greeted by his Father and Mother, there was a tremendous crack of light like the most fearsome lighting strike and noise that shook the foundations of the earth once again. The darkness, this strong evil presence from the pit of damnation was crushed down and broke into a million pieces like droplets falling from the sky it was gone that quick, destroyed with such power and intensity it shattered it back into the depth of hell from where it came. Its power had gone its hold had been destroyed the mob were reeling with the pain in their ears and blinded by the intense light. But they had no more hate in them and were not controlled but were confused about where they were. Most of them turned back and started to walk away back into town some just sat and were perplexed and bewildered. They started to disperse and shake their head wondering about disoriented.

Stephanie was crying she could not help it; she saw what had happened and knew the darkness was gone. She watched as Richard was stood with his parents still and silent. She looked around and smiled, then felt a strange presence, a strong powerful but loving presence. She turned looked right into the face of her mother who was stood by her side. The feeling over whelmed her and she cried, her mother walked forward and took her in her arms they hugged and the feeling of her mother's touch empowered her with love and happiness.

"I am so sorry" she said in a low voice looking her mother with tears in her eyes.

"You have nothing to be sorry about you have freed me and I am now in a perfect happy place, you go live your life and know I am always with you my little angle" she smiled and it glowed and made Stephanie smile she was happy and knew now her mother was free and happy. They hugged and stayed there holding each other.

Richard looked at his Father smiling at him and his Mother stood next to him, there was no pain or fear in their eyes, they were happy and healthy.

"I miss you both" He said looking at them in turn.

"Go and have a happy life son, live it with Stephanie I always knew she was a special child, you too are now free, you can go live your life, the evil is gone and will not come for you again I promise you that" she smiled in a warm and wonderful way, we will always be by your side and watching" his mother said. They all hugged and stayed like that until slowly they faded and suddenly they were gone. He looked round and could see Stephanie wiping tears from her eyes they looked at each other and didn't know what to say at first. Max whimpered and came up to his master he was confused and didn't know or understand what was happening.

"We are safe, my mother is safe" Stephanie said smiling. They both looked up and round the church it was still and just a church now but they always knew it was a special place and would always be a special place to them, to the ones who knew.

The church was still and was quiet, the day was peaceful now and calm, no one was around. The place was composed and a very special place. It was a place where people were at peace and lived happily. No one could see them no one could hear them but they were there, safe and secure blissful and content.

This very special place had been here for a very long time, Angels walk here, it is a powerful place and no darkness could penetrate it. No evil could ever exist here, it was a holy place a good place and a secure place.

The sky lark was singing its song chirping away continually so high in the sky, raising up and up higher and higher eventually it was just a dot up so high looking down. Richard smiled as they walked out into the sunshine. Looking up he listened to that sky lark and it took him right back to his childhood. He was stood with his childhood sweetheart and the future looked good and happy for them both.

The End

Kev Carter

Printed in Great Britain
by Amazon

27268065R00126